BOOK TWENTY-EIGHT

The pampered only child of a prominent London surgeon, Paula believes her happiness will be complete as soon as she can get Barnabas Collins to propose.

But it is the evil Dr. Nicholas Bentley who first offers marriage. Paula refuses indignantly; Bentley's unsavory habit of buying corpses from grave-robbers has made him the scandal of the medical profession. And from that moment, Bentley becomes a vengeful enemy bent on turning Paula into a zombie and destroying Barnabas forever....

Hermes Press

Published by Hermes Press, an imprint of
Herman and Geer Communications, Inc.

Daniel Herman, Publisher
Eileen Sabrina Herman, Managing Editor
Kandice Hartner, Production Manager/Senior Graphic Designer
Erica McNatt, Copy Editor/Graphic Designer

2100 Wilmington Road
Neshannock, Pennsylvania 16105
(724) 652-0511
www.HermesPress.com; info@hermespress.com

Book design by Eileen Sabrina Herman
First printing, 2022

LCCN applied for: 10 9 8 7 6 5 4 3 2 1 0
ISBN 978-1-61345-254-7
OCR and text editing by H + G Media and Eileen Sabrina Herman
Proof reading by Eileen Sabrina Herman and Feytaline McKinley

From Dan, Sabrina, and Jacob in memory of Al DeVivo

Acknowledgments: This book would not be possible without the help and encouragement of Jim Pierson and Curtis Holdings

Printed in China

Barnabas, Quentin and the Grave Robbers
by Marilyn Ross

CONTENTS

CHAPTER 1

At dusk on a gray day in March, 1830, Paula Sullivan pushed aside the blue drapes of her bedroom window to gaze out at Widenham Square. The big town house in which she and her father lived was located in a fashionable section of London and the activity in the square reflected this. An elegant carriage had halted at the mansion next door and a footman was helping a lady, whose brown bonnet matched her full-skirted velvet dress, from the vehicle.

Paula smiled to herself. She recognized the woman as the wife of Tracy Henderson, an eminent barrister, who owned the house. Prunella Henderson set the fashion for their social group and she was a friendly if somewhat talkative young woman, a good deal younger than her husband. Gossip had it she was a flirt but Paula didn't think there was any harm in her. Both Prunella and her husband were to be guests at a dinner party being given by Paula's father that very evening.

A trace of fog was beginning to close down on the rooftops of the city. In a little while the yellow-gray mist would become dense enough to wet the streets and make it difficult to see. The street gaslights would loom eerily in the foggy night and travel in the great city would become more difficult and vastly more dangerous.

Paula hoped the fog might not be too bad; she wanted the dinner party to be a success. It was being given in honor of a visitor from America, Barnabas Collins. At the mere thought of the handsome, charming man Paula's face brightened. She was a beautiful twenty-two with a wistful, oval face and fine intelligent features. Her large brown eyes and shining light-brown hair, which she wore coiled at her ears, were her best features. She had met Barnabas at a party given by a friend and almost instantly fallen in love with him.

At the moment he was the most popular single man in all London. No social event was complete without him; young women vied for his company. Because of this, Paula knew it was a personal tribute to her that he had agreed to come to her father's dinner party. She had been seeing him with some frequency and fortunately her father approved of the quiet, charming man.

As she gazed out the window other carriages moved across the square in a constant flow of traffic. A few people were walking, and a purveyor of oranges and other fruits pushed his cart before him as he paused every so often to cry out the merits of his wares to the houses along the way. As Paula watched a maid came scurrying out of one of the houses to rush across to the peddler and make a purchase.

There was a light knock on the door of Paula's elegant, high-ceilinged bedroom and she went over and opened it. Standing there resplendent in a black silk dress was Aunt Lucy, her father's spinster sister, who had acted as mistress of the house since the death of Paula's mother. Paula had been a baby of seven months when her mother died, so Aunt Lucy was the only mother she knew.

The older woman had a long horse-face and was rather tall. But she had a dignity, enhanced by her gray hair and a crisp, pleasant manner. Waving her ivory fan, she entered the room and took stock of Paula in her crimson gown.

"I see you are dressed, my dear," she said. "You look lovely."

"Thank you," Paula smiled and dutifully kissed her aunt on the cheek. "So do you."

"At my age one attempts only to be presentable," the plain woman said. "Your father is downstairs ready to welcome our guests. I think we should join him."

"You go on," Paula said. "I'll be down in a few minutes. I want to do a bit more with my hair."

Aunt Lucy studied her. "Don't bother with it too much. It looks very well now."

Paula moved over to her dressing mirror, a huge oval of glass with a golden frame. She eyed herself in it and was also able to observe her aunt standing in the background. She said, "I won't be long."

Aunt Lucy looked wise. "I can guess why you're primping so

much. It's because that Barnabas Collins is coming."

She smiled in the mirror. "I want to look well for all our guests."

"But especially for Barnabas," her aunt said. "There was a time you thought only of John Williams."

"John Williams is a doctor and I vowed never to marry a doctor," Paula said, touching a brush to her hair. "It is enough to be the daughter of one. And in any case John is married now, and to a very wealthy girl."

"I know he is married and that Jane is wealthy," Aunt Lucy said. "But John is still very much in love with you. He can't hide it."

"Nonsense," she said lightly, though she believed it was probably true.

"John will be at the party tonight and I can imagine he'll be jealous of the attention you're bound to be paying to that Barnabas."

Paula swung around to face her aunt, the brush still in her hand. "But why should he be jealous of me? A married man! Why should he care what I think of Barnabas?"

"I've told you," her aunt said with a knowing expression on her long face. "John Williams will always love you regardless of who he married. And you might have done better to have taken him as a husband rather than trying to get this Barnabas Collins to propose."

Paula's cheeks went as scarlet as her dress. "Don't you approve of Barnabas? Father likes him."

"Your father is so wrapped up in his surgical practice he isn't half aware of what is going on, or what people are saying." Aunt Lucy drew herself to full height. "But I hear things!"

"What things?"

"I hear this Barnabas, in spite of his charm, is a rather shadowy, mysterious character."

"That's silly!"

"Wait a minute," her aunt said. "I have been told that he lives in a most disreputable part of London, which is strange since he is supposed to be a young man of wealth and family."

"Barnabas prefers the company of the more colorful slum people," Paula said. "He lives in a poor district to study its inhabitants."

"Indeed?" Her aunt raised her eyebrows. "And why does he wish to study them?"

"He is considering writing a play about them."

"And that's another thing," Aunt Lucy told her. "He associates with theater people—and some of them young women of very questionable reputations."

Paula gave the older woman a scornful smile. "Now that is merely gossip. Of course Barnabas frequents the theater and knows many actors and actresses. There is surely no harm in that."

"Some think so," Aunt Lucy said soberly. "Theater people are not at all desirable."

"Unless they be the pets of royalty," Paula said with annoyance. "Then all doors are opened to them. How I hate this hypocritical London society!"

"Still, you are part of it. And so you are expected to obey the rules."

"That, I refuse to do," Paula said, incensed.

"Another thing. No one ever sees this Barnabas in the daytime. They say he carouses the entire night and sleeps all the day. A servant answers the door of his lodgings during the daylight hours and allows no one to see him."

"Is there anything wrong in his sleeping during the day?"

"Nothing wrong, perhaps," Aunt Lucy sniffed. "But most peculiar!"

"That is what I find your attitude," Paula said. "Most peculiar!"

Aunt Lucy relented. "I'm not trying to annoy you, child. I'm only attempting to protect you. If there is any question about the character of this Barnabas Collins I don't want him around you."

"You need not worry. Barnabas is a fine person."

"But dissolute in his habits," Aunt Lucy said. "You must accept that."

"You don't understand him," Paula protested. "So few people do. I'm glad that father approves of him. And he knows everything you've told me. He is aware that Barnabas lives in slum lodgings and has many associates from other worlds than ours. But he also realizes that as a journalist and would-be playwright Barnabas must seek a wide view of society."

Aunt Lucy snapped her fan shut. "We can't stand here all night discussing the merits of Barnabas Collins," she said. "We have other guests to think of."

Paula looked worried. "Barnabas is a fine person. I'm sure of it."

"You're in love with him," her Aunt said despairingly. "Naturally you'll find no wrong in him."

"But he is a good man," she said. "You'll find out."

Her aunt was at the door. "I promise to be nice to him," she said. "But if I get an opportunity I'm going to quiz him on some of his friends. If he is going to court my Paula he must be discreet in his associations." And having said this the older woman went out and closed the door.

Paula sighed and turned to the mirror again. She wished her aunt wouldn't be so critical of Barnabas. It was true he didn't fit into the mold of the conventional nice young man. He was more mature and he had standards of his own, too broad-minded for Aunt Lucy ever to approve or understand them.

After working with her hair a few minutes more, she went to see how much worse the fog was, before joining her aunt and father in receiving their guests. It was darker as she stared out the window again, and the fog had become thicker. She could barely see the other side of the square. The gas lamps along the square had been lighted and the fog cast an orange halo around each of them. She lifted her eyes in time to catch a glimpse of a huge, strange bird which came swooping out of the fog, brushing against the pane of the window.

She started back in alarm. The thing swooped off again and circled to return close by the window. This time it flew on by and she had a good glimpse of it. Fear surged through her at the thought that it resembled a bat! She had a dread of bats and she'd never seen one so large . . . nor had she encountered one in the city. Her only experience of them before had been in rural Sussex where her father's cousin had a farm. Once she had been caught in the hayloft as one swooped close to her, upsetting her so much that she could not join the other children with whom she'd been playing a game of hide and seek.

She'd nearly fallen down a ladder leading from the hayloft as the thing had flown around her, squeaking eerily. She was terrified it would dart in her eyes or hair. In the end she'd escaped, of course, but the fright of the experience remained with her.

She let the drape fall back in place and tried to blot the picture of the huge bat from her mind. She wanted to be at her best when she went downstairs. She mustn't dwell on her strange experience. Probably no one would believe her if she told them; they would insist it had been a large crow or something. With a sigh, she started for the door.

Some of the guests had already arrived and were standing in the elegant white and gold foyer chatting and drinking the strong punch which footmen were passing around. She went to join her father and her aunt in the reception line.

Aunt Lucy gave her a critical glance. "I can't for the life of me see that your hair looks any better for all the extra fussing."

Her father, Sir Phillip Sullivan, spare, graying and aristocratic in appearance and demeanor as befitted London's leading surgeon, took her hand in his and smiled. "Pay no attention to her. You look beautiful."

"Thank you, father." Paula smiled back. "There is a lull in arrivals for a moment."

Her father nodded. "And not too many more to come."

She glanced around. "I see Barnabas hasn't arrived yet."

"Never fear, he'll be here," Aunt Lucy said bleakly.

At that moment John Williams and his wife, Jane, arrived. A pleasant young man with a square, determined face, John had risen from a modest background to become a highly successful doctor. At his side, in a rose and ivory gown of a rich brocade was Jane, a fragile, winsome young matron with straw-colored hair.

They were greeted by Sir Phillip and Aunt Lucy, and then Jane paused to smile demurely at Paula. "Your dress is so becoming," she murmured.

"And yours, as well." Paula always felt a little self-conscious with the wife of the young man who had so long made no secret of his romantic interest in her. Even though John now made his declarations jokingly, she knew he more than half-meant them.

As Jane moved on, John seized her hand with a warm smile. "Paula, how lovely you always are! But then, you know you still have more than a half-claim to my heart!"

Paula blushed and hoped that his wife had not heard. She said, "It is good to see you again, John. Be sure that your wife gets some punch."

"We must talk later in the evening," John said, still studying her admiringly.

"Of course," she said, and dismissed him with a smile. He was forced to move on, as the couple from the mansion next door, Tracy and Prunella Henderson, had arrived. Prunella, a vivacious redhead, gave Paula a smile and a quick wink as her elderly husband lingered to exchange pleasantries with Aunt Lucy.

Prunella said, "I notice your long-time admirer still pays you tribute, in spite of his having married."

Paula smiled at the young matron. "We are still good friends."

"There is much of that going around the town, I know," Prunella teased her. Then she moved on.

Tracy Henderson, dried up at sixty, took Paula's hand in his emaciated one and touched his dry lips to it. His thin, wrinkled face wore a look of pleased triumph. He fancied himself as a ladies' man and his marriage to young Prunella had caused tongues to wag.

"Another party in Widenham Square," he wheezed. "I say we can't have too many of them."

"I'm so glad you and Prunella were able to come," she said.

"Prunella was at her grandmother's on the other side of town, and I feared she would be very late," the old lawyer said. "But she managed to get here earlier than I expected."

"How fortunate," Paula said, hoping that Prunella wasn't playing tricks on the old man.

At this moment Barnabas Collins arrived. He wore a black opera cape which he allowed a servant to take and his dark evening clothes were of the smartest cut. Sir Phillip gave him a warm handshake. Aunt Lucy was less friendly in her greeting, but pleasant enough. And then the handsome, gaunt Barnabas came to take her hand.

As Barnabas took her hand, she noticed his was cold to the touch, as always. And his lips, when he kissed her hands, were also ice cold. She had often wondered about this. His burning, deep-set eyes fixed on her.

"What a beauty you are," he said in his resonant voice.

"I began to fear you wouldn't get here."

He smiled. "Miss an opportunity of seeing you? You should know better."

"I will soon be able to leave the door," she said. "Then we can talk a little before dinner. I've missed you."

"I have had a good deal to do," he said. "My plans for presenting my play are almost made."

"You must tell me about it," she said. And then she noticed a tiny jade watch fob hanging from the pocket of his vest. It was a carving of what surely appeared to be a bat! She eyed it and asked, "Where did you get that?"

He looked at it and smiled. "In America," he said. "I knew someone who had a deep interest in bats."

She gave a tiny shudder. "They terrify me!"

"They're not all that bad," Barnabas said, the deep-set eyes watching her closely.

"Perhaps not," she said. "But I had an odd experience tonight. One came flying close to my window. I've never seen them in London before."

"No doubt there are many of them here."

"Perhaps," she agreed. "You know Tracy and Prunella Henderson, don't you? Why don't you talk with them for a little, until I'm relieved of my hostess duties here?"

Barnabas nodded pleasantly and moved on toward the table with the huge cut glass punch bowl and the footmen serving the refreshment. Paula was about to ask her father if she could retire from the reception line, when another guest arrived—one who filled her with uneasiness.

It was Dr. Nicholas Bentley, a surgeon of wide reputation about whom there had been many grim whisperings. He was supposed to be completely without scruples and her father had been in open opposition to him. Paula had met him several times before when she'd gone to Winslow Hospital to meet her father. She couldn't imagine why he had been invited to this select gathering of friends for a formal dinner.

Bentley gave the servant at the door his hat and stick and

then glowered at the assembled company. He was extremely tall, well over six feet, with graying hair and a prominent hooked nose. His eyes were shrewdly narrow and the lips of his long, grim visage were thin. Heavy gray eyebrows drooped over the narrow eyes.

As he advanced stiffly to her father she could sense the veiled hostility between the two men. Her father introduced him to Aunt Lucy and then he came to greet her.

He bowed and took her hand in his. "Miss Sullivan, how delightful to meet you again," he said in his harsh voice.

"It has been quite a while."

He held her hand a moment longer than was quite agreeable, and she noticed how hairy and claw-like his hands were. It struck her as somehow wrong in a surgeon. Her father's hands were delicate and free of hair. She found herself not following what he was saying for a moment.

"You will know many of our guests," she said faintly.

He smiled coldly. "Yes—though I am not of the same social level as your father and am not invited around widely. In my early days surgeons were regarded as no more than barbers. Times have changed!"

"I had no idea," she said.

He continued to smile. "I can tell you much about the profession. And I should like to. I trust we may come to be good friends."

"Thank you," she said uneasily. She knew Nicholas Bentley was a bachelor with a reputation for being interested in young women much his junior. She hoped he was not becoming attentive to her.

"No doubt your father has told you how occupied my profession keeps me," Bentley went on. "But I do have a fine carriage and a prize matched pair of grays. It would be a great pleasure to call for you one day and take you for a drive."

"Thank you," she said. "I rarely go anywhere without Aunt Lucy."

His narrow eyes showed a gleam of annoyance. "In that case I should think you lead a restricted social life."

The arrival of a last guest, an elderly physician, forced Dr. Bentley to move on. Paula greeted the old doctor, happy that his entrance had rescued her from the boorish surgeon.

At dinner she sat between Barnabas and John Williams. Although both men were interesting conversationalists, Paula gave most of her attention to Barnabas. Once she happened to look up and see Dr. Nicholas Bentley across the table glaring at her. It was plain to see the middle-aged surgeon was jealous of the two younger men. She felt this was ridiculous and again wondered why her father had included him in the dinner party.

Barnabas smiled at her and said, "I hear you occupy much of your leisure doing charity work. Your name is known for your good deeds in the area in which I live."

Flattered, she blushed. "I do what I can," she said. "I would rather help the poor than devote myself exclusively to afternoon tea and gossip in a friend's drawing room."

"You deserve credit for that," Barnabas said approvingly. "This London of ours is a city of devastating poverty as well as wealth. I have learned that since I came here."

"In America you lived in a small village, didn't you?" she asked.

He nodded. "Yes. A place in Maine along the shore. It is called Collinsport. Our family's estate, Collinwood, is a few miles from the village."

"Do you miss it?"

His face shadowed. He looked suddenly gaunt. "Yes," he said, "I do."

Aware that he felt deeply on the matter, she became curious about his reason for leaving home. "Why did you decide to come to London?"

Barnabas looked grimly amused. "Fate plays strange tricks on us. There are times when we cannot control our destiny. I felt I must leave Collinwood, but I plan to return."

"I hope you do." She smiled. "I can tell you're lonely for it."

"Yes," the handsome man agreed. "But then, I also like travel and cities. When I was in America I spent a great deal of time in Boston. And I surely like London. I'm also no stranger to Paris or Rome."

She listened with growing interest. "I hear you always travel with a servant," she said.

"I have had several," Barnabas said. "All mostly the best of fellows. At the moment I have Will Loomis. He guards me well."

"So I hear," she said. "A friend of mine tried to visit you one day and this Loomis wouldn't allow her inside the door."

Barnabas chuckled. "He was obeying orders. I'm abroad much at night and prefer to sleep during the day."

John Williams leaned forward to question him. "What is this business of your sleeping all the day?" he asked. "That's hardly normal, is it?"

Barnabas shrugged. "It suits me. I'm sorry if it upsets others. I must live my life as I decide."

Williams looked piqued. "You can afford it; you have no wife or children. If I attempted to do it I'd be dubbed a selfish, inconsiderate swine!"

She turned to John Williams with a reproving smile. "You can hardly compare yourself with Barnabas. He leads an entirely different life."

"And he is welcome to it," John said grumpily. And in a lower voice he added, "Why do you neglect me to prattle so gaily with him?"

Paula blushed. "I wasn't aware that I had."

"You have," he said. "And what's more, you're making that churlish chap across the table angry—the tall brute with the long, ugly face and slit eyes."

She knew he meant Dr. Bentley, who at the moment was engaged in a serious discussion with the elderly physician on his left. She told John Williams, "That is Nicholas Bentley, the famous surgeon. He works in the same hospital with father."

John said, "I'd hate to have him cutting me. He seems cruel enough to really enjoy it!"

"John," she protested and turned to Barnabas again. When dinner was over, the ladies went to the drawing room for tea while the men remained around the table for brandy. After a little the men, led by Paula's father, came trooping into the drawing room.

Sir Phillip smiled at his guests after they'd seated themselves or found a comfortable spot to stand, and informed them, "My daughter will now entertain you at the pianoforte."

Paula rose, somewhat embarrassed, to polite applause from the group. She advanced to the pianoforte and sat before it. She considered for a moment before deciding to play a favorite minuet. The group were quietly attentive and she moved on to several other pleasant selections from the really good composers. The candles flickered in their tall silver sticks and Barnabas stood close to the piano, encouraging her with one of his sad smiles.

As Paula got up from the pianoforte she saw Dr. Bentley and her father talking. Bentley appeared displeased about something; his face was very angry and once he turned to give her and Barnabas an ugly glance. After a moment she saw her father walking out to the entrance hall with the tall surgeon, apparently still arguing with him. Paula was glad to see him leave the party.

She and Barnabas were standing in a corner of the drawing room away from the other guests. She watched her father vanish with the evil-looking colleague and gave a deep sigh.

Turning to Barnabas, she said, "I fear Dr. Bentley has not enjoyed his evening. He is leaving early. But I must admit I'm not sorry."

Barnabas lifted his black, arched eyebrows. "I have had an eye on him all the evening. He appears a surly fellow."

"He is much more than that, I fear," she said, her pretty face shadowing.

Barnabas smiled at her mockingly. "I have an idea he is interested in you and angry because you avoided him. You will note that he left without trying to say goodnight to you."

"I hope he does know what I think of him," she said indignantly. "At least I won't be embarrassed by his offers of carriage rides."

"Aha," Barnabas said. "I knew he must have been giving you attention."

"It did him no good," she bristled. "I'd rather go out with John Williams, who is presentable and nice, even if he is a married man."

"I trust that rules him out."

"It does," she assured him. "Jane is my good friend. I would certainly not flirt with her husband."

Barnabas had a twinkle in his deep-set eyes. "I hope that leaves me as the only contender for your hand—no, that is an idle conceit. All the young men in London are in love with you."

Paula played demure. "My first loyalty is to my father. He needs me here."

"But the day will come when you must choose a husband," Barnabas pointed out.

Her reply was stifled by the sudden reappearance of her father, who looked actually ill. Although he managed to smile and nod to his other guests as he passed them, his aristocratic face was ashen.

He came up to Paula and Barnabas and touched a hand to his temple. "My attempt to placate Bentley by showing him hospitality met a grim failure," he said in a shaken voice. "You saw him leave just now."

"Yes," Paula said worriedly. "Why did you ever invite him here?"

Her father sighed. "I hoped that here in my home, treating him as a friend, I might be able to reason with him. I should have known better."

"He's a surly scoundrel," Paula said indignantly. "I'm glad he has gone."

Barnabas was staring at her father. "I can see that he must have distressed you greatly, sir," he said.

Sir Phillip nodded bleakly. "Just before he left, he threatened my life!"

CHAPTER 2

Paula gasped, "How dare he do such a thing!"

Her father looked grim. "And I can promise you that he meant it. He has given me a warning that if I continue to cross him he will see that I am murdered."

"What sort of man is he?" Barnabas asked, his concern evident. "And why has he become so enraged at you? You are both members of the staff of Winslow Hospital, aren't you?"

Sir Phillip's aristocratic face had lost some of its pallor. Glancing back to his other guests in the far section of the huge drawing room, he said, "They seem to be entertaining themselves very well. Lucy will see to it that they have plenty to drink and the party is kept moving. I think we may safely go off for a private conversation in my study. We can use this door; they won't see us."

He led the way out of the room. Paula gave Barnabas a concerned glance and they followed him down a short dark passageway into the paneled study where Sir Phillip spent much of his time when at home. He closed the door after them and waved them to easy chairs.

Sitting at his desk, a frown on his face, he asked Barnabas, "Would you know what I meant if I told you our surgical friend, Dr. Nicholas Bentley, is a patron of the resurrectionists?"

Barnabas smiled grimly. "Are you hinting he is a religious

fanatic? He doesn't strike me as one."

"Not at all," Sir Phillip said. "A resurrectionist is a term we use for those active in supplying bodies for dissection. The scarcity of bodies for anatomical study has given rise to a particularly gruesome type of criminal, the grave robber."

Paula added, "And Dr. Bentley never asks questions, but buys bodies from the foulest ruffians!"

"Grave robbing has become a profession," Sir Phillip said grimly. "The resurrectionists are familiar figures at the back doors of medical schools. And I believe the situation has gone further than that. That these scoundrels are murdering people and selling the bodies to the medical profession!"

Barnabas was listening intently. "I have heard rumors about this. But never the facts."

Sir Phillip's aristocratic face showed disgust. "There must be laws passed to stop the incentive for this crime. Medical schools should be able to receive a proper supply of bodies for dissection. For the most part we get only those of persons who have committed suicide or been publicly executed, with a few from the Potters' Field, the bodies of the poorhouse dead."

Barnabas said, "I think we have had the same problems in America."

"Indeed you have," Paula's father said. "Though I understand there is an anatomy law in Massachusetts. Under this law the coroner is authorized to dispose of the bodies of men killed in dueling either by burial, 'without a coffin, with a stake driven through the body, or to deliver the body to any surgeon or surgeons to be dissected and anatomized.' It seems even in these instances dissection is regarded as deplorable and a penalty inflicted on those caught dueling to the death."

Barnabas' gaunt face had taken on a strange expression. "I have had some experience of this brutal business of a stake being driven through the heart of a corpse. I would banish it as both cruel and criminal."

Sir Phillip nodded. "Except in the case of vampires, the walking dead. You know the only way to destroy them is by a stake through the heart."

Distressed, Paula said reprovingly, "Father, there are no such things as vampires! That's a legend."

"I fear you are wrong there," her father said. He glanced toward Barnabas, "Don't you agree?"

Barnabas didn't reply for a moment. His handsome face was shadowed. In the light of the flickering candle from the mantel his features looked more gaunt than usual.

At last he said, "I dislike setting myself up as an authority. I have had certain personal experiences which would lead me to have an open mind on the subject."

"You see," Sir Phillip told Paula. "Even as clever a man as Barnabas does not scoff at the possibility of there being vampires. Indeed, several of our London hospitals have had cases of young women with strange marks on their throats and almost total amnesia. This only recently. They have recovered and in nearly every instance they recall being attacked by a dark, vampire figure."

Paula shuddered. "Don't talk about such things! You terrify me!"

"I'm sorry," her parent said. "As a doctor's daughter I thought you were hardened to gruesome tales."

Barnabas gave her a look of understanding. "I think you are right. We were discussing the nefarious Dr. Bentley and the resurrectionists. Let us stay with that."

"By all means," Sir Phillip said. "You may have heard of the violent outburst against dissection in New York in the so-called Doctors' Mob of April 1788. On that day Dr. Richard Bayle, working in the laboratory of the Hospital Society, observed a small boy peering in at one of his windows. In a spirit of medical humor he waved the arm of a cadaver at the boy to frighten him away. The terrified lad spread exaggerated tales about the incident and a mob formed and marched to the building and burned the anatomical collection. The physicians of the hospital took refuge in jail. The jail was attacked and the militia had to be ordered out to quell the riot. Seven were killed and others badly injured. The following year the legislature of New York authorized the dissection of the bodies of persons executed for burglary, arson and murder."

Barnabas seemed extremely interested. Leaning forward in his chair he said, "And so things have still not improved much. Bodies remain difficult to obtain for dissection even in this year of 1830."

"Indeed they do," Sir Phillip said. "You must have read of the Scottish resurrectionists, Burke and Hare. Three years ago in Edinburgh they undertook a series of murders to obtain bodies to sell to medical schools and doctors. They perfected a method of murder known as 'Burking' in which one partner held the victim down while the other smothered her by holding his hands over her nose and mouth. This way they avoided any marks on the body to give rise to a suspicion of violent death. They peddled their victim's bodies for around ten pounds."

Paula, prettier than ever in the subdued candlelight of the study, said, "Of course they were eventually caught."

"Yes," her father agreed. "Hare turned state's evidence and Burke was hanged last year before a crowd of some twenty thousand.

After the execution the mob attacked Dr. Knox, who had bought many of the bodies, and his school. His life was saved only by the police arriving in time. Dr. Knox was technically innocent, but he must have known that the bodies were not legitimately obtained."

"Just as Nicholas Bentley does," Paula said bitterly.

"Exactly," Sir Phillip agreed. "Knox was ostracized and finally had to leave Edinburgh."

Barnabas said, "And you fear Bentley may bring disrepute to Winslow Hospital?"

"And the profession generally," Sir Phillip said, a frown on his aristocratic face. He rose from his desk and began to pace up and down. "I have made charges against him at the hospital and that is why he is so incensed. Still he continues dealing with thugs who he knows must be robbing graves or murdering to supply the large number of bodies he has been buying."

Barnabas looked grim. "One would have hoped that at least the grave might be a sacred resting place for weary humanity. Now these vultures despoil this last sanctuary."

Paula said, "It's dreadful! We have heard stories of bodies being buried only a few hours before they are dug up and stolen by the grave robbers. Mourners come the next day to pay their respects and find a hole in the earth and an empty coffin facing them."

Sir Phillip halted his pacing to say to Barnabas, "You can imagine the distress caused by such a discovery."

"Indeed, I can," Barnabas said bleakly.

"There is a good deal of gossip about Bentley," Sir Phillip went on. "You saw by his appearance and behavior here tonight that he is a strange person. Even though he is quick with the scalpel, he is heartless in surgery. Of course he has saved many lives but I suspect he has also lost more than a few."

Paula gave a tiny shudder. "I noticed his hands tonight. Like hairy claws. I don't think of them as surgeon's hands!"

Her father stood before the fireplace with the candle on the mantel casting a glow on his patrician face and mane of white hair. "I'm convinced Bentley is engaged in some experiments that go far beyond the realms of ordinary medicine. He has a laboratory in an old brick mansion on the edge of the Wexley slum district and not too far from the hospital. The medical students who work there with him are a strange lot. And he has a huge, brown-skinned servant who guards the place. His name is Jabez and he is supposed to have come from the West Indies. Voodoo has been mentioned as part of his background… some have whispered that this Jabez is actually a zombie."

"A fit servant for a grave robber," Barnabas said. "A dead man without soul."

"Please!" Paula protested.

"In any case, Jabez keeps unwanted visitors out of the place," Sir Phillip said. "And so it is hard to say what may be going on there. I'm sure he's conducting some weird experiment."

"And they say Bentley heads a circle of Black Magic worshippers," Paula added.

Barnabas gave them both a concerned look. "It would appear you are dealing with a thoroughly evil man."

"He made that clear tonight," the surgeon said worriedly, "when he ordered me to cease my criticism of him or be prepared for violence against myself and my family."

Barnabas frowned. "Was he hinting that Paula might also be in danger?"

Sir Phillip hesitated. "I'm afraid so."

"I'm quite willing to take my chances along with you, Father," Paula said resolutely.

"And you feel you must continue to oppose Bentley in spite of his threats?" Barnabas asked Sir Phillip.

The aristocratic face of Paula's father showed pain. "I have no choice. I wish I had. As a member of a profession dedicated to humanity, I cannot sit idly by and let Bentley blacken the reputation of all medical men."

"You're right, Father," Paula said.

Barnabas gave her a troubled glance. "This could lead to serious trouble for you," he said. "You must be extremely cautious in the future."

"I'll see that she is," Sir Phillip promised. "I have told you my story, Barnabas, in the hope you may be able to help. You live in an underworld section of the city. It is possible information about what is going on may come your way. If so, I wish you would pass it on to me."

"You may count on that, sir," Barnabas said.

"Thank you," Sir Phillip said, seeming less worried. "I'm lucky to have another associate at the hospital who is in this fight with me, John Williams. He has joined me in my stand against Bentley, whereas most of the rest of the staff prefer to close their eyes to his iniquity."

"John Williams should make a good ally," Barnabas said.

"So now I should return to my guests," Sir Phillip sighed. "But I wanted to tell you the full story and ask for your support before the evening ended."

Barnabas rose. "I'll be glad to do anything I can."

Paula, also on her feet, smiled wanly at him. "See how much trouble being a friend of ours can bring you?"

Barnabas smiled back. "There are times when I find trouble

a challenge." Together they returned to the drawing room, where the party was still in progress.

Paula said goodnight to Barnabas about an hour later. He was among the last of the guests to leave. And when all had gone and she started up the broad curved stairway with her father, she saw how haggard and weary he was.

"You look dreadful, father," she worried. "I hope you haven't to be at the hospital too early in the morning."

"All I need is some sleep," he said with a tired smile. "You mustn't worry."

"You know I will."

"Be careful here," her father said. "When you and Lucy are in the house alone, be wary. And never go walking by yourself."

She frowned. "What a rigid set of rules we must live by."

Her father's concerned gray eyes met hers. "I know that Nicholas Bentley wasn't talking idly," he warned her. "And I noticed he was watching you closely all evening. He may hope to strike at me through you."

"You mustn't worry about me," Paula said, taking his arm as they continued up the stairs. "I'm glad we have Barnabas on our side, and John Williams."

At the doorway of her room, her father kissed her goodnight. She went inside, feeling upset both about his unusual fatigue and the danger they were facing. She began to slowly prepare for bed. Her personal maid, a lively young girl named Emma, had waited up for her, and now she darted around the room putting clothes away, preparing the bed and helping Paula with her toilet.

As Paula sat before the dresser mirror brushing her long brown hair, Emma remarked, "It was a marvelous party, Miss Paula. Me and the second cook peeked out from the back hall and saw all the men and women in their fancy clothes."

Paula smiled at her. "I think you had the best of it. Being with the guests all the time was tiring. I'm sure my father is worn out."

"Poor Sir Phillip!" Emma said sympathetically. "He does look weary these days and no mistake."

"Perhaps when the summer comes we'll go to the country for a little," Paula said hopefully, as she gazed at herself in the mirror.

"That would be good," the maid said. "I believe the fog has lifted a mite."

And she went to the window to gaze out. She pulled back the drapes and stared down into the square below. "Oh!" she said sharply.

Laying aside her hairbrush, Paula turned to the girl. "Is something wrong?"

"I don't know, miss," Emma said, still gazing down at the

square. "But there's a strange man down there. I don't like his looks at all. And he seems to be staring up here."

She rose from the dresser and crossed the room. "Let me see."

Standing down in the street and gazing blankly up at Paula's window was the most extraordinary giant of a man she had ever seen. He was huge—not only tall, but broad. He wore no hat and she could tell that his skin was dark. His face was expressionless and his eyes had a dead look. He stood there like a stone figure looking up toward her—yet the weird eyes seemed unseeing. At once she thought that it must be Bentley's servant Jabez, who so many whispered was a zombie!

Frowning, she asked the maid, "Have you ever seen him here before?"

"Not him!" Emma said in a hushed voice.

"I wonder how long he's been there and what he wants."

The maid looked scared. "Should I rouse the butler, Miss? Mr. Ebbets will put him in his place and send him away. The police shouldn't allow him to behave like that. But then, where can you find a policeman on the London streets after dark?"

Paula was still studying the motionless figure of the giant brown-skinned man. With a shudder, she said, "He must be mad!"

"He stands there staring at us and not seeming to see us at all," the maid said nervously.

Paula closed the drape and moved away from the window. "He wasn't out there when Barnabas Collins left. He must have come after our guests had gone. Someone has sent him here."

The maid hovered near her. "He could be a murderer, miss. There's plenty about after nightfall. We could all have our throats cut in our sleep!"

She patted Emma's shoulder. "Don't think too many wild things, Emma," she said. "He seems to be a West Indian. Perhaps he is only a drunken sailor who has lost his way to the docks."

The maid looked pale. "He's wandered a good bit if that's the case."

"I may have to speak to my father about this," Paula worried. She knew her parent would recognize Jabez, if he should be the stranger standing out there. "See if he is still there, Emma."

The maid scurried back to the window and peeked out. "He's gone!"

"Are you sure?" She went over to check for herself. Staring down into the darkness she saw that the square was empty.

On the following day, in the late afternoon, Paula was seated in the sewing room working on a fancy shawl for herself when

Ebbets, the butler, came to her with a disdainful look on his thin face.

"Someone at the door wishes to speak to you," Ebbets said. "I tried to take the message but he wouldn't give it to me. What shall I do, Miss Sullivan?"

Paula was on her feet at once. "I'll speak to him," she said, putting her sewing aside. "It may be important."

"He is rather a low type," the butler warned her.

She smiled at him. "You mustn't be so snobbish, Ebbets. You know I do a great deal of charity work among the poor."

"Yes, miss," he said quietly and stood aside for her to go to the door.

She walked quickly along the tiled hallway and when she reached the door Ebbets, who had followed her, opened it for her to reveal what was surely one of the scruffiest specimens of human kind she had ever seen. Stooped, dirty and scrofulous-looking, the man leered at her with the toothless gums of his ugly face revealed in what was intended to be a smile. Reaching inside the filthy, ragged jacket he wore over equally ragged breeches he produced a neatly folded note.

"For you, miss," he said. "Compliments of Mr. Barnabas Collins."

Paula gingerly took the note from his dirty hand. She was astonished that Barnabas should use such a messenger, but then he did live in a slum section of London.

She stared at the scarecrow of a man. "Do you know Mr. Collins?"

He nodded vigorously. "I often see him in the tavern under his lodgings. He gave me threepenny to see this safely delivered."

"Thank you," she said. And she opened the note to read the short message, "Come to 24 Cannon Lane at once. I have discovered something about Dr. Nicholas Bentley. And come alone. This is most important, Barnabas."

"Is there a reply?" the ragged man asked.

She raised her eyes from the note with a frown. "No. I think not. I'll be going down to visit Mr. Collins. Can you tell me where Cannon Lane is?"

"I can that, miss," he said. "It's situated just two blocks from where Mr. Collins has lodgings. You go through an arch and down a narrow side street. Anyone down in the East End will tell you."

"Very well," she said. And she waited for him to leave.

He eyed her with his bloodshot eyes and, rubbing a hand over his beard-stubbled chin, said, "Should you want an escort, I'd be willing."

She studied him with disgust. The thought of being in the filthy man's company shocked her. "No," she said carefully. "I'll be going down there later."

"Yes, miss." He shuffled uneasily. "Well, I guess I'll be on my way."

All at once she realized he was waiting for more money. So she turned to Ebbets, who'd been standing quietly in the background, and asked him, "Can you provide me with a shilling, Ebbets?"

The butler raised his eyes. "Why, yes, I believe so," he said. And he produced a wallet from an inner pocket and dug for the coin. He produced it after a moment and passed it to her.

She, in turn, handed it to the ragamuffin. He at once brightened.

"Thank you very kindly, miss," he said happily, his smile again revealing pus-swollen gums. With a nod he turned and hurried down the steps and off across the square.

Paula watched him go with confused feelings. Ebbets came to close the door after their unusual guest. She told him, "Thank you. I'll see you are repaid the shilling, Ebbets."

The butler showed no smile. "That was quite all right, miss," he said. "Is that all?"

"Yes," she said. "That will be all."

After he'd left her alone in the bright foyer she reread the message and tried to make up her mind what to do about it. Of course there was only one thing to do. Barnabas had sent her an urgent message and required that she keep it strictly a secret. She must go to him at once.

She went back to the sewing room and gathered up the things she'd had there, then went upstairs to her own room, being careful as she passed Aunt Lucy's room not to waken her from her afternoon nap. She put on a red bonnet and cloak and took some money from a box in her dresser. Thus provided for, she went quietly down the winding stairs and slipped out the front door to the steps.

In a moment she was in the bustle of Widenham Square, at large in the great world outside her father's home. She recalled guiltily that he had warned her never to go out alone, but she'd had no choice. Now she paused in the bustle of the cobblestone street to hail a carriage.

At last a shabby one came to a halt by her and she asked the bleary-eyed, red-nosed driver, "Do you know the way to Cannon Lane?"

Perched on his seat behind the carriage, the driver said, "And if I did, why would a nice miss like you be wanting to go there?"

Already Paula felt embarrassed standing in the middle of the fashionable street with stares coming her way from all directions. She quickly drew out a banknote and thrust it at the driver.

"Will you take me there?" she asked.

His eyes were greedily fixed on the note. "In a jiffy," he said. "Get in." And he snatched the money from her.

Paula quickly opened the rusty-hinged carriage door and got inside. The interior was as miserable and unprepossessing as its outside. The cushion was broken down and moldy; there was a reek of strong liquor. She hastily opened the window to let some air in and sat back bracing herself, as the ancient vehicle clattered over London's cobblestones.

She should have confided in someone, she thought anxiously. Surely Barnabas would not have been angry if she'd brought her maid along for company. Emma could be counted on to say nothing. But it was too late now.

When she engaged in her charity work she always went with other young women from the church, and often one of the church elders accompanied them. They were never alone. Now she was being driven to one of London's most poverty-stricken and dangerous districts. Still, when she found Barnabas she'd be safe.

The streets grew narrower and shadowed. The carriage had to halt every so often for pedestrians in the cramped area. There were harsh shouts from outside as the driver exchanged bellowed insults with the drunken or stupid in the way of the vehicle. Paula glanced out the window in time to see a blowsy female seated on the steps of a stone house, holding a gin bottle to her lips.

She was almost at the point of opening the small slit in the rear of the carriage and requesting the driver to turn back, when the vehicle came to a jolting halt, and the driver peered through the slit to inform her, "This is Cannon Lane, miss. You sure you don't want to be driven back to Widenham Square?"

"Quite sure, thank you," she said, trying to appear calm. She struggled with the door until it opened and she stepped out onto the filthy cobblestones of the narrow street.

The carriage rolled on, leaving her there alone. Dusk was starting to draw in... or, at least, so it seemed there in the alley-like street. Two scrawny children came up and stared at her as if she were a visitor from another world, which indeed she was.

Quickly turning from them, she walked a few steps along the hovel-lined alley until she came to the arch. She remembered receiving the instructions to go through the arch in order to find number twenty-four; it was almost like entering a tunnel.

An old man came lurching up to her, muttering to himself and staring at her with rheumy eyes. He looked poverty-stricken but relatively respectable. So she asked him, "Can you tell me where I'll find twenty-four?"

"Twenty-four?" he repeated slowly in a thin voice, peering at her.

"Yes. Twenty-four." She wasn't sure he had taken it in or was capable of taking it in.

He swallowed hard and then pointed a skinny forefinger to a door a dozen paces away on the left "That's it!" he said. "That's where Hoskins lives."

"Thank you," she said.

"If it's a body you're wanting to buy, he can arrange it as quick as anyone," the old man chuckled. "I'd best keep moving or he'll be after my poor one." And he moved on.

Paula was in no mood to enjoy his joke as she started down the shadowed alley. She could only assume that Barnabas had come upon this headquarters of the grave robbers and was waiting there for her to reveal their secrets.

Now she reached the battered plank door of number twenty-four and rapped on it. There was no reply so she rapped again. When no one answered her second knock she tried the door and it opened. Inside was black and dank.

She took a few steps in the shadowed dingy hall and then called out, "Barnabas!"

There was no reply. But as her cry echoed down the dark hall the door behind her was suddenly slammed closed and out of the shadows between her and freedom loomed the huge, monstrous Jabez!

CHAPTER 3

The unexpected appearance of Dr. Bentley's servant told her everything in a flash. She had walked into a trap. Terrified, she slowly retreated until she touched a wall of the nearly black hallway. Then she screamed.

Jabez moved slowly toward her like a sleepwalker, his eyes still blank and apparently unseeing. But he came directly to her and seized her roughly. She screamed again as he lifted her effortlessly and took her along the passage.

Suddenly a door opened at the end of the corridor and some light showed. Outlined in the doorway was the stooped, filthy scoundrel who had delivered the note to her.

As Jabez carried her toward him, she recognized him and cried out, "Help me! Where is Barnabas?"

The filthy one seemed to think this a fine joke. He chortled and told Jabez, "Bring her in here to me and Mary. That's the good fellow!"

Jabez propelled her into the small, dirty room and let her go. She fell forward on the floor sobbing as the huge, ghostly figure retreated in the shadows of the corridor again.

The toothless ruffian smiled and closed the door. "Come now, miss. There's no need to go on so," he said in his harsh voice.

Paula had gotten to her feet, and she faced him indignantly.

"What kind of game are you playing? Where is Barnabas?"

He chuckled. "The name is Hoskins, miss. Samuel Hoskins, Esquire. Welcome to me humble abode!"

"Is Barnabas here?" she demanded.

"He was detained," Hoskins said. "That's it! Detained!"

"I don't believe you!"

This appeared to amuse him. "Not believe Samuel Hoskins? You are a one!" He chortled again.

She gazed around the tiny room with fear and misery on her pretty face. What she'd taken to be a pile of old rags began to stir in the corner and the form of a stout, ancient female revealed itself. The old woman wore a dirty bonnet over a wrinkled, sodden face and gazed at her from under puffy eyelids.

Sitting there on the wretched mattress, the old crone inquired of Hoskins, "And who is this quality miss what has come to visit us?"

"Miss Paula Sullivan," he said, introducing her. "The daughter of the surgeon, Sir Phillip Sullivan."

The crone hooted. "So be it! You're all in the same profession!"

Hoskins smiled crookedly. "You might say I was at the underground end of it!"

"Underground end of it!" the crone repeated hilariously. "That is good!"

Hoskins looked at Paula modestly and explained, "This lady is an associate of mine. One-Eyed Mary, they call her. If you'll look close you'll see one of her eyes is clear glazed over. But she's a handy skirt in my line of business. She will clean up a cadaver and send it spotless to the medical schools by way of me. Not many enjoy that line of work."

Paula stared at him with revulsion. "You're one of the vultures who roam London, robbing graves and worse!"

"If it weren't for chaps like me, where would people like your father and Nicholas Bentley be?"

"My father has never had trade with the likes of you!"

Hoskins shrugged. "Maybe so, maybe not. You have to have a market for goods, even when the goods are corpses!"

"Why did you lure me here?" Paula demanded.

The crone on the mattress cackled. "Maybe one of his doctors needs a pretty corpse for his students. They pay a fancy price for that sort!"

Sheer terror surged through Paula. "Please, let me go!" she begged.

Hoskins eyed her derisively. "Now you should know better than that, after all the trouble I went to in order to get you here. I was afraid you wouldn't swallow what was in that note the doctor wrote.

But he was right. You did."

She backed away a little. "Dr. Bentley masterminded this diabolical scheme?"

Hoskins shrugged. "You can be sure I wasn't itching for your company, miss. At least not while you're still breathing!" And he laughed at his own joke and turned to One-Eyed Mary for an audience.

The crone didn't let him down. "That's right," she said, choking with laughter. "I swear Hoskins never takes a second look at a woman unless she's dead. Or anyone else, for that matter!"

Paula decided to try another approach. She told Hoskins desperately, "I'm worth much more to you alive than dead. Let me go. Take me back to my father in Widenham Square and he'll pay you a handsome ransom. I guarantee it."

A crafty expression of greed crossed his dirty face, and for a moment she thought she might have accomplished something. Then his expression became wary. "No use," he said. "I owe too much to Bentley. And he's the one who'll pay me best for keeping you here."

"My father or Barnabas will find me," she warned Hoskins. "You're making a grave error!"

The old crone shrilled mirthfully from her mattress, "All his errors are of the grave!"

Hoskins joined in her laughter at this sally. "She's a smart one," he said.

Paula tried to hold back her tears as she asked, "What is it you want of me?"

Hoskins looked wily. "It's not what I want, miss, but what the doctor wants. Bentley means to settle accounts with your father. And he needed you as a hostage to do it."

"You can't aid him in this wickedness!"

Hoskins sat heavily on a nearby stool. "A man of my age and bad health has to take what comes along. Bentley has been a good employer. He never asks questions as long as I do as he tells me. He told me to get you down here and I've done it."

One-Eyed Mary struggled up from the mattress. She was an incredibly short and dumpy woman. "Where's the gin?" she demanded.

Hoskins shot her an ugly glance. "There ain't none! You drank the last of it! You should know!"

The crone studied him balefully with her single good eye. "You're lying as usual. I brought my bottle with me. You've taken it!"

Hoskins jumped up. "Call me a liar under me own roof?"

"That's what you are!" she shrilled back.

"Get out!" he shouted in his gravel voice. "And don't you come back until you're willing to ask me pardon!"

The crone drew herself up in an almost comic fashion. "It's easy to see who you want to be left alone with and why," she said. And to Paula she added, "You'd better watch him close, miss!" And with this baleful warning, the old woman tottered over to the door and went out.

"Miserable old drunkard!" Hoskins remarked in disgust.

Paula had backed to the wall and was watching him now with fear-filled eyes. He moved over to a cupboard in the corner and produced a nearly full bottle of gin which had undoubtedly been brought there by the old woman.

He grinned at Paula. "I'd rather share it with you than her."

"No," she said tautly.

"Think yourself too good to drink with the likes of me, eh?" Hoskins sneered. "Well, I'll have my bit of it anyway." He lifted the bottle to his lips, took a swig, and then smacked his lips. He proffered the bottle to her again, "Sure you won't have a drop?"

"I don't drink gin," she gasped, sickened at the thought of drinking from the bottle that had just been poked in his pus-ridden mouth.

He grinned meaningly. "Maybe you will before you're finished," he said. "Maybe you'll be glad to have a drink then!"

His words brought her new terror. She was certain Dr. Nicholas Bentley was determined to degrade and harm her in some awful fashion. In his twisted mind she and her father were his enemies; he was planning to make them pay an awful price.

Hoskins seated himself on the stool again and stared up at her. He kept the bottle of gin in his hand. "A spot of this goes well on a winter night in the graveyard," he said. "That's the time to get a body. When it's too cold for anyone to be around. But it's not a comfortable line of work and the ground is hard to dig. So you take a splash of the nippy stuff and you manage a lot better."

She tried to control the tremor in her voice as she asked, "Is Dr. Bentley coming down here?"

Hoskins grinned. "I expect so. He didn't say. He just sent Jabez with the message that I was to go get you and keep you down here. He sent the note along that was to be the bait and I delivered it to you."

"What is wrong with Jabez?" she asked.

The stooped, filthy one gave her a wink. "He's strong enough, ain't he?"

"He seems demented!"

"Does his master's bidding," Hoskins said. "Never talks or asks questions. He came from one of them voodoo islands. Like a walking dead man he is. A slave to Dr. Bentley."

She stared at the grave robber. "You're saying that he's some kind of supernatural creature?"

Hoskins nodded. "That's it, miss. Back in those heathen islands they rob the graves of the dead and do better than just dissect them like the doctors do here. They take the corpses and bring them back to a kind of life. The kind Jabez has."

"I don't believe it!"

"You'd better. Those witch doctors know a trick or two. And Dr. Bentley had them get Jabez for him when he visited the West Indies a few years ago. Jabez has been his slave ever since."

"He's just simple-minded, not a body raised from the grave," she said. "There are no such things as zombies."

He gave her another of his sly grins. "And maybe you don't think there are vampires either?"

"Of course not!"

"I'll tell you better," Hoskins said. "I've seen vampires. And I've known those who have been bitten by them and escaped with nothing but a scare, and a few who weren't so lucky—they turned into the living dead too."

"Nonsense!"

"There's a female lives a few doors away is a vampire." Hoskins spoke so seriously that she was certain he believed it. "Sleeps in her neat little coffin by day and roams around at night. Name of Lily. Cursed the same way your friend Barnabas Collins is."

Paula gasped. "What are you saying about Barnabas?"

Looking delighted, he took another swig from the bottle. "I thought that would get you!"

"You're lying!"

"Not a bit of it," Hoskins said, pointing a dirty forefinger at her. "Everyone in this part of London knows why Barnabas Collins lives here. Of course he's a great gentleman, but he's been cursed as a vampire. And so he hides down here in his coffin by day and at night he leaves his lodgings to wander all around London."

"Barnabas will make you pay for those stories about him when he finds out," she warned him.

Samuel Hoskins showed a grim smile. "Maybe I'll have a chance to prove I'm telling the truth. So when you gave your heart to Barnabas you gave it to a monster, almost the same as Jabez."

"No!" She put her hands to her ears to shut out his hateful words.

"He's one who likes to walk about in graveyards too," the man went on. "More than once I've encountered him in a field of tombstones and wished him a pleasant good evening—him there to feel comfortable among his own kind and me looking for a fresh one that had just been covered with six feet of earth. Everyone to his own line. That's my motto. Live and let live. If Barnabas wants to go about drinking the blood of young girls, let him do it!"

"You can't poison me against Barnabas with your cruel lies," she protested indignantly. "Look, all I want to do is leave. Can't you--"

She broke off as the door burst open and One-Eyed Mary stumbled into the room.

"Coppers!" she shouted to Hoskins. "Coppers coming down the Lane and heading for here!"

"Blimey!" he gasped, jumping up and dropping the gin bottle which rolled across the floor. The old woman uttered a cry of delight and pounced on it. At the same instant Jabez came stalking into the room. Hoskins gripped him by the arm and cried, "Get her out of here! Take her to Lily's!"

"No!" Paula screamed and darted toward the door.

It was hopeless. Jabez could be swift when he liked, she learned. He seized her with cruel roughness. One huge hand pressed over her mouth to cut off her screams and his other arm held her body close to his huge bulk as he rushed out into the dark hall with her again. She could hear Hoskins and the old woman jabbering in the distance.

Jabez was taking her in a different direction this time. They went down some steps and out into a yard. Even as she struggled she was aware that it was night. Darkness had fallen. Jabez crossed the yard and entered a door so low he had to stoop to get inside with her. Then he carried her up a flight of stairs.

She was on the verge of fainting but somehow managed to retain her senses and an idea of where she was. Jabez paused on a landing and then mounted a second flight of stairs, so mean and narrow that he stumbled more than once in the darkness. Next he climbed up what seemed like a ladder and they emerged from the fetid hallways to the fresh air again.

New horror came to her as she realized Jabez had carried her onto a rooftop. A peaked roof with a dangerous slant, at that. He held her struggling body with ease as he crouched against a tall chimney and looked down into the street. There were shouts and people running back and forth. Paula could make none of it out clearly but vaguely realized the police must be making some sort of raid on the grave robbers.

Jabez remained there by the chimney for a little. Then he got to his feet, and still holding her close, slithered down the slanting roof and leaped to an adjoining one. He reached a sky light and went down in it, dragging an almost limp Paula after him.

They went down a flight of stairs and he paused before a door. Then he opened it. A candle flickered on a plain plank table, giving the room a ghostly air. Jabez opened another door and dropped her on the floor of a small side room. Then she heard him turn the key in the lock of its door. His heavy footsteps faded off as he left this new place he'd taken her.

Her rib bones ached from his grip on her and her head was throbbing wickedly. She dragged herself across the floor of the stuffy, dark room until her back was braced against the wall. She knew she must be several buildings away from number twenty-four where Hoskins had held her prisoner, but that was all she could deduce about her new place of captivity.

A slit of dim light showed under the door from the outside room; her eyes were gradually becoming accustomed to the near darkness. As she peered into the shadows around her, she was startled to discover she was not alone!

Her heart pounded with excitement and fear. In a far corner someone sat on the floor of the bare room in a position not unlike her own. It looked like a girl. A slim girl.

She called out. "You there!"

There was no reply, nor was there any motion from her companion sharing the bare room. She called out again, "Please, speak to me! Say something!" She thought she could guess why the other young woman didn't reply; no doubt she was even more terrified than was Paula.

Paula struggled to her feet. Touching a hand to the wall as she moved around the nearly dark room, she went over to the girl in the opposite corner.

"You needn't be afraid," she said. "I'm a prisoner here, too. We'll get away somehow." The girl still made no reply.

Paula peered down at her in the darkness. The girl was young and plain of features. She was staring straight ahead of her with an unhappy expression on her thin face. Paula bent to her and touched her cheek. Then she went rigid with terror. The girl's cheek was cold, lifeless! This was a corpse!

"No!" she screamed in wild panic and stumbled back.

She moved as far from the forlorn corpse as she could. Then she began to pound on the door and scream to be let out. Her screams turned to sobs, then silence. There was no response.

Slumping to the floor, she leaned against the door and prayed that she would be released before her sanity left her. She averted her eyes from the girl's corpse, which was surely awaiting delivery to Dr. Nicholas Bentley.

Had the unfortunate young woman been murdered? Was she some hapless streetwalker lured to the flat and murdered as Burke and Hare had murdered their prey? Or had she succumbed to some loathsome disease whose germs were still infecting the dark room? Paula didn't dare dwell on it.

She tried to think about the police. Tried to make herself believe that they had come to her rescue and were even now searching for her. It seemed to her that she had discussed 24 Cannon Lane with Hoskins when Ebbets was standing in the background. Surely after she was discovered missing the butler would recall the visitor and the discussion of Cannon Lane. But everything depended on whether Ebbets had taken in the details or not.

What would her father be thinking at this moment? Would he be calling on John Williams and Barnabas for aid? There could be no doubt of that. And it might be that the police she'd seen and heard in the streets had come in search of her.

There were voices from the outside; she scrambled to her feet in a surge of hope. And then she recognized the voices as those of Samuel Hoskins and One-Eyed Mary and her heart sank again. From the other side of the door she heard Hoskins ask, "Where is she?"

The crone cackled. "Maybe he dropped her from the roof and her body won't be worth a farthing!"

Preferring even their company to that of a corpse in this dark room, she pounded on the door once again. "I'm in here!" she cried.

There were quick footsteps towards the door, the key twisted in the lock, and then the door was opened by Samuel Hoskins.

"So Jabez put you in there!" he said.

"In with the body of that girl," One-Eyed Mary observed.

Hoskins reached in and grabbed Paula. "You don't belong in there yet," he said. "Plenty of time for that."

She stumbled out weakly, hardly able to stand, but said defiantly, "The police are here. You'd better let me go. They'll catch up with you."

Ignoring her comment, Hoskins helped her into a chair. "There you are! That's better!" And he went back to lock the door of the room the corpse was in.

The crone poked her ruined face into Paula's. "You've got a lot to learn, dearie," she said.

Hoskins returned and pushed the crone away. "Let her be!"

"I was only trying to help," she whined.

"You can do that best by minding your own business," he replied harshly. The old woman murmured something and went over to a cot in a corner of the room and stretched out on it.

Paula was beginning to feel somewhat better. She said, "You can't fool me. I know why you brought me here so quickly. The police are after you!"

Hoskins sneered at her. "They were. They've left now, without finding anything at all."

"They'll be back."

"Not for a while." Hoskins shuffled across the room to stare disgustedly at One-Eyed Mary. "She's rotten with gin!"

"She would have to be, to work with you," Paula said. "You murdered that poor girl in there to sell her for a few pounds, didn't you?"

"That poor thing died sudden," the stooped one said in mock sadness.

"You made it sudden," she said. "I only hope that Barnabas catches up with you. He'll see you pay for this."

Hoskins smiled nastily. "I might take a notion to visit his lodgings one afternoon and plunge a stake through his heart. That would finish your Barnabas."

"Don't be ridiculous!"

"You'll find out," Hoskins said.

She was losing hope fast. She could tell by Hoskins' confident behavior that the crisis was at least temporarily over for him—and she'd not been rescued.

Suddenly the door to the flat opened and a young woman came sauntering in. Paula stared at the newcomer… another of her jailers? She was wearing a blue skirt and a low-cut blouse. She had dark fuzzy hair and a thin but not unpleasant face, with thick lips painted heavily. Her eyes and eyebrows were also made up and her cheeks rouged in distinct circles, so that she looked more like a corpse than a human being.

She paused with her hands on her hips and stared at Paula. "What have we here?"

Samuel Hoskins turned to her uneasily. "I didn't expect you back this early."

The woman shrugged. "I couldn't stay out in the streets with the police swarming around."

"They're gone now," Hoskins reminded her.

"I know it, but they put me off, just being here." She eyed Paula with a kind of professional appraisal. "Who is she?"

"A girl Bentley wanted me to bring here," he said.

The woman gave him a mocking smile. "So now he has you procuring live bodies for him along with dead ones."

"No." Hoskins frowned. "You have it all wrong. You never get anything straight, Lily."

Lily. Hoskins had mentioned Lily when he'd been discussing vampires. And he'd insisted this woman was one.

Lily smiled at her scornfully. "You don't look very happy, dearie."

"Make him let me go," she appealed to the painted woman.

"Maybe you ought to do that," Lily said to Hoskins. The stooped man shook his head.

"No chance of that. Bentley wants to talk to her. She's staying the night."

Lily raised her eyebrows. "Then she'll need a place to rest. She can have one of the beds in my room."

Hoskins gave her a knowing smile. "You're very generous all of a sudden, ain't you?"

Lily drew herself up haughtily. "I lower myself to associate with scum like you."

Hoskins chuckled. "It's because you can do no better you're here. Let's not talk about you. If you want to give a bed to this girl, it's all right with me."

The woman gave her a sympathetic glance. "You're tired, honey," she said. "Come along to my room. I have an extra bed."

Hoskins stood by Paula's chair and ordered her, "Go on. You'll be safe with Lily."

Lily pouted at him. "The question is will I be safe with her? From the looks of things, she's put up quite a fight to escape."

"I'll be on the alert out here," Hoskins said. "And Jabez is around."

"I might have known that," Lily said grimly. She helped Paula out of the chair. "You come with me," she said, in a friendly tone.

Paula hesitated, facing Hoskins. "You won't change your mind and let me go? I promise not to give anything away about you. I'll not say anything."

The stooped man shook his head. "You stay here until Bentley says different."

"Come on, girl," Lily said, and she led her across the room to another door which opened into a small bedroom with sloped ceilings and two narrow-sized beds in it.

Paula suddenly realized how exhausted she was. She gave the painted woman a woeful glance. "Why don't you help get me out of here? If you'd take a message to my father or Barnabas Collins they'd rescue me."

Lily's eyes widened strangely. "Did you say Barnabas Collins?"

"Yes," Paula said. "He's a friend of mine." She stared up at the woman looming over her in the dimly lighted room. "What's wrong?"

Lily didn't answer. Instead she stretched out her long, claw-like nails toward Paula and seized her. Opening her mouth, she revealed long fangs at either side. She bent quickly to kiss Paula on the neck and sank the fangs deep into her. Paula screamed and screamed but gradually she became weaker and a curtain of blackness descended on her.

CHAPTER 4

The room gradually came into focus. Paula's head was still reeling and she felt strangely weak. Awareness returning, she discovered she was on the cot in the corner of the room, where One-Eye Mary had thrown herself earlier. There was a tingling at her neck and she lifted her hand to touch the spot.

Then she remembered. A vampire kiss! She'd lost consciousness almost at once. She turned her head and saw Jabez seated by the cot.

His big brown face impassive, he stared straight ahead of him in that odd way of his. His hands hung down on either side of the chair and only the clenching and unclenching of his fingers indicated he was alert and ready for any emergency.

She raised herself on an elbow and the blur of the room cleared enough for her to make out Samuel Hoskins, One-Eye Mary and Lily seated at the table a distance away. She blinked her eyes in an effort to clear her vision. Jabez turned his shaven head slightly; she felt any sudden motion on her part would bring a quick reaction from him.

Lily turned and saw that she was sitting up. "You feeling better, luv?" she asked in a sympathetic tone.

Paula was afraid of her but didn't want to show it. "Yes," she said in a low voice.

Lily gave Jabez an angry glance. "You're not needed here!" she told him. "Go!"

The huge brown man hesitated, then rose from the chair and marched out of the room, still gazing directly ahead of him like a sleepwalker. In a moment the door closed after him, and Lily took his place at Paula's side.

"You don't need to be afraid of him, luv," Lily assured her. "I'll see he doesn't hurt you."

Paula pressed a hand to her cheek and tried to collect her thoughts. "Can I leave now? Why am I being kept here?"

The woman leaned close to her and in a low voice said, "It's Hoskins who's to blame. He's keeping you here for that doctor."

"It's mad!" Paula said, near tears.

Lily patted her on the shoulder. "Don't you give up, luv. It will turn out all right. You could be worse off. Like the one in there." And she nodded her head toward the door of the side room where Paula had encountered the corpse of the young girl.

"My father will find me," Paula said. "It will only be worse for Hoskins the longer he keeps me here."

Lily sighed. "I can't help you, luv. You know what I am. When the dawn comes I'll be like your friend, Barnabas, asleep in my coffin."

Fear came into Paula's eyes. "Why do you speak of Barnabas in that manner?"

"Because it is true, luv," Lily said with a sad look on her painted face. "Barnabas and me both suffer from the same curse. There are many of us haunt the dark London streets."

"I don't understand," Paula fretted.

"Better that you shouldn't."

Their conversation was interrupted by Samuel Hoskins, who shuffled up to them. He gave them a sly look and, smiling toothlessly, said, "So you two have become proper friends?"

Lily stiffened. "What's wrong with that, Sam Hoskins?"

Hoskins shrugged. "Not a thing. I'm one who minds my own business." And to Paula, he said, "You must be weak and weary. The doctor doesn't want you ill treated. I'll get you a cup of warm cocoa."

At this moment Paula was so weak and thirsty that the offer sounded appealing, despite the dirt and squalor of the surroundings. So she made no protest and Hoskins shuffled away to prepare the cocoa.

Lily told her, "Don't try to fight back. It will be better if you don't. Hoskins can be mean and cruel if he wants. Just pretend to get along with him until you have a chance to get away."

Paula looked up at her with begging eyes. "Couldn't you get a message to Barnabas for me?"

"I could but I won't," Lily told her bluntly. "I know when I'm well off. Hoskins would toss me out of here if he found out and where could I go? You don't have any idea how hard life can be, luv."

"You seem basically a good person," Paula said.

The woman smiled grimly. "Thanks, luv. I feel kindly toward you. Some of your blood is in my veins now. But there is only so much I can do."

One-Eye Mary came creeping up and cackled at Paula, "So now you're a sister to a vampire! Hoskins ought to approve of that! It means you're almost half dead!"

Lily turned on the crone angrily. "You leave her be!"

"You want her all to yourself!" the old woman snapped back.

"Never you mind about that," Lily said, arms akimbo. "If you want your hair pulled out, just keep on as you are!"

One-Eye Mary glared at her with her single pale blue eye. "I'm not afraid of the likes of you! I'll come to your coffin in the day and put a cross on your bosom and a stake through your heart!"

"You old harpy!" Lily said, grabbing her and shaking her angrily.

"Leave me be!" the crone shrilled.

"Ladies! Ladies!" Sam Hoskins said, stepping up between them and pushing them apart. "Is that any way for you to behave?"

"She started it!" Lily cried. "The gin-soaked old biddy!"

One-Eyed Mary smacked her lips and shook with rage. "Don't you call me that, you vampire!"

"That will do!" Sam Hoskins said sharply. "I want you both to get out of here for a while. This young lady and me has things to talk over. And we don't need the likes of you to eavesdrop!"

Lily gave Paula a troubled glance. "I'll see you later, luv," she said. "And remember all I told you." With that she pulled her shabby shawl about her and went out.

Hoskins turned to old Mary. "Well?" he asked. "You heard what I said."

"It'll soon be dawn, Sam," the old woman protested. "Me bones are weary. I'll sit in the corner and not say a word. Don't put me on the street."

He gave her a warning look. "All right. Just see that you do keep quiet. Or else out you go!"

"Thank you, Sam," the old woman murmured and she crept back across the room to the chair in the far corner.

With the steaming cocoa cup still in his hand, Hoskins smiled at Paula broadly. "The ladies often give me a spot of trouble. Females is hard to get along with, agreed?" He handed her the cocoa mug. "Wonder this didn't get cold while they were having their fuss."

She took the hot cup from him and sipped it. It tasted good. She said, "This is madness, keeping me here!"

"Not really," he said. "I'll warrant the doctor knows what he's doing. He'll be coming to see you tomorrow. Meanwhile, I want you to get some rest. I'll be leaving shortly and Mary will stay to keep you company." He winked at her. "I have an important package to deliver before the sun rises." And he jerked his head in the direction of the side room where the corpse was.

Paula attempted to stifle her repugnance for him and her surroundings, so that she could down the cocoa. She required the nourishment it offered. She went on sipping the pleasant beverage and she could almost feel her strength coming back.

She said, "When can I talk to Dr. Bentley?"

"He works in his home operating room every night. It will be sometime tomorrow. But he'll come. He has a special interest in you."

"I must get away from here."

The sly smile came back to his beard-stubbled, ugly face. "No use you trying to bribe me or start any of that again. I've thrown my lot in with the doctor and there can be no changing of that."

Paula finished the cocoa and put the mug down. Arguing would take too much effort. An overpowering feeling of sleepiness surged through her, overwhelming everything else. She had never felt so sleepy before.

Hoskins wavered before her. She tried to see him clearly as she said, "I'm sleepy. Very sleepy!" And she was startled by the sound of her own voice, she was slurring her words like a drunken person.

"That's my lovely girl," Hoskins cooed with delight. "You have yourself a nice sleep."

A vague feeling of alarm flashed in her mind. "Drugged," she said in her strange, thick voice. "You drugged me!"

Hoskins was helping her settle back on the cot. "I want you to have a good rest, dearie. Just you relax. You'll feel better when you wake."

She was drifting off to sleep, fighting it and yet unable to do anything about it. She gazed up at him with heavy-lidded protest. "You!" she managed in an accusing tone. But she could go no further. Her eyelids closed and she at once sank into a deep sleep.

Later as the drug began to wear off, Paula began to experience a series of nightmares. She once again was dragged across the rooftops by Jabez. They slipped and stumbled on the roofs of ancient buildings with the streets a dizzying distance down below them. One false step would send them both crashing down on the cobblestones. And then Jabez fell and let her drop!

She was hurtling down through the air, screaming out piteously. In a matter of seconds she would be a bloodied corpse sprawled on the cobblestones. Not even the resurrectionists would want her body. But a miracle happened: she floated down onto the cot and One-Eye Mary was standing over her with a gloating smile on her puffy, wrinkled face. The blind eye stared in another direction while her good eye was fixed on her.

Paula saw the small stake and mallet in Mary's scrawny hands. "What are you going to do?" she demanded in terror, sitting up.

"You're a vampire now, dearie," the old woman cooed. "I'm going to drive a stake through your heart!"

"No!" Paula screamed.

Then she was running down a long dark hall and the weird, monstrous Jabez was loping after her with hands outstretched to seize her. She glanced over her shoulder as she raced on and saw that he was close and looked at the horror of his blank face and sleepwalker's staring eyes. She screamed! Then he caught her by the arm and she went on screaming!

Sitting up with a start, she was still screaming as she came awake on the cot. Seated beside her bed with a supercilious expression on his hawklike countenance was a richly-dressed Dr. Nicholas Bentley.

"You have been suffering from a nightmare," the thin lipped man told her.

Hope came into her pale face. "You've come to free me."

His smile was cold. "Did I say that?"

"No. But you must have!" She sat weakly on the edge of the cot.

"You shouldn't jump to hasty conclusions," Bentley said, an evil gleam in his slit eyes. "I had you brought here."

She saw that they were alone in the room. "Why?"

"You should know why."

"To revenge yourself on my father?"

Bentley smiled coldly. "That's part of it."

Paula said, "He is only standing up for what he believes is right. You shouldn't be bartering for bodies with cutthroats and thieves. At the best, they are robbing graves and at the worst, murdering!"

Bentley fastidiously removed a piece of lint from his trouser leg. Then he glanced at her and informed her, "My work is more important to me than anything else. I don't care where the bodies come from. I must have them."

"You must be insane!"

"Dedicated is the word," Dr. Bentley said. "And if I lived in Widenham Square and had a title like your father, no one would say a word. They would turn their eyes from what I'm doing and pretend none of it was going on. I happen not to have a social position, so I'm unfairly treated!"

"That's nonsense," she argued. "John Williams and other doctors feel the same way about you my father does. They feel you're disgracing the profession of surgery."

The doctor looked grimly amused at this. "John Williams is bound to agree with your father. He is in love with you."

"John is a married man. I'm a friend of Jane's. What you say is nothing but nonsense!"

"You may think so but I know differently," Bentley said in his maddeningly calm fashion.

She stood up. "I demand that you release me at once."

"Don't excite yourself," Bentley said, remaining in his chair. "And don't try to make a break for the door. Jabez is standing just outside it, waiting for you."

She took a deep breath. "You threaten me with a madman!"

"Jabez is far from mad."

"He is not normal!"

"I disagree," the doctor said with a thin smile. "He is completely normal in almost every way. But he lives only to do my bidding. I act as his brain. He is a product of the voodoo doctors of the Indies. They raised him from his grave and offered him this new life. I was able to purchase him from them and bring him back here with me. I have never regretted the purchase."

She stared at him. "I think you must be the insane one!"

"I'm sorry you feel like that," he said, his eyes showing a mocking gleam. "I've been hoping that you would like me!"

"Like you! After you have me kidnapped by this crew of thieves and killers!"

"Ah, but I had a reason," he pointed out. "I'm infatuated with you."

This left her breathless. "Infatuated?"

"Without a question," he said, one hand leaning on his fashionable ebony walking stick. "And this suggests a plan which would make us all happy."

"I don't want to listen to it," she said, turning her back on him. She was more frightened than ever before.

"You had better," he said calmly. "I would like us to be married before I free you. As my wife you would offer me a new position socially. And your father would not dare to make his accusations against a son-in-law. He would be forced to keep his opinions to himself."

She turned on him angrily. "I would rather die than marry you!"

He showed mild interest. "I will give you that choice."

"What?"

"If you prefer not to be my wife then I shall have Hoskins prepare you as a cadaver for dissection at the Winslow Hospital Medical School."

She vividly recalled the body of the young girl in the side room. Horror crossed her pretty face. "No!"

He smiled cruelly. "Can't you picture it? I'll have you delivered just prior to one of your father's anatomy demonstrations. He'll have his students gathered around him as he lifts the sheet from the body on the marble table. Then he'll see it is you. His beloved Paula! Imagine his horror and pain!"

"Don't say such things!" she begged.

"Perhaps he'll even take a stroke there at the table. The sight of his beloved daughter prepared for dissection by the specialists Samuel Hoskins and One Eye Mary. The scene delights me."

"You'd never dare!"

He rose languidly from his chair. "You think not?"

"My father would see you on the gallows!"

"Your father would not be able to prove any connection between your murder and me," he told her.

"He knows who Hoskins works for!"

"But to prove it would be most difficult," Bentley said. "Now how do you feel about my marriage proposal?"

"I despise you!"

He flinched and spots of red appeared on his cheeks. "Really? I think with a little persuasion you might become fond of me. Who knows? I'm willing to give you a day or two longer to make a decision."

"I'll never marry you."

He moved toward the door. "If you still feel that way in a day or two, I'll turn you over to Samuel Hoskins' care. You understand what I mean by that."

"You'll have my father and John Williams to deal with," she warned him. "Not to mention Barnabas Collins, whose name you used to lure me down here. Wait until he finds out about that."

"I doubt that he will find out," Bentley said in his overbearing manner. "The only one who could tell him is you. And you will never leave here alive unless it is as my wife."

"I'd rather die."

"A curious choice," he observed calmly. "Still, you are entitled to it. I'll return tomorrow afternoon or night. Maybe by then you'll have had a change of mind."

She stood with her fists clenched at her sides. "Never!"

"Good day, Paula," he said with a smile. "Be assured that you are always in my thoughts." And with this mocking farewell he went out into the dark hallway and shut the door after him.

She slumped down on the cot and began to sob bitterly. She knew he was capable of carrying out his threats and had meant every word he'd said.

What to do? She'd been gone almost a full twenty-four hours now and no one had come to rescue her. It seemed only too likely that Ebbets had not properly overheard the address or had forgotten it. Her father and Barnabas would have to comb all London to find her. And they'd never manage it in time.

"Don't you want to be a bride?" It was One Eye Mary who put the question to her.

She lowered her hands and looked up to see the old crone standing by her. "You heard him?"

"Part of it."

"I couldn't marry him! I loathe him!"

"A girl needs a husband," One Eye Mary croaked. "And an old woman needs gin. I wonder what's keeping Sam Hoskins with that bottle." She glanced nervously toward the door.

"Hasn't he returned yet?" she asked. Hope was rising in her. Perhaps her father had been waiting for one of the resurrectionists to turn up at the medical school with a body and then he had seized him and questioned him about her. He might even have Hoskins in his hands at this moment.

Mary smacked her lips and said, "No. He took a bit of goods to the medical school and he was supposed to return right away. He's like as not in a tavern drinking up his profit along with mine."

Paula studied the evil old woman and could see that she was very uneasy. If Jabez hadn't been outside, she would have grappled with the crone and attempted an escape. She said, "Maybe the police have him."

The crone looked terrified. "No!"

"They likely have," Paula insisted. "And if so, they'll be here soon. You could save a lot of trouble by helping me escape."

The old woman cackled with bitter laughter. "They'd twist my neck for that!"

"Not if you came along with me," Paula said. "I'd take you to my home and give you a room in the servant's quarters." She paused. "And I'd see you always were supplied with plenty of gin."

The single good eye of the crone lit up. In a hoarse voice, she said, "You would?"

"I promise."

The crone hesitated as if considering. Then she said, "No. Hoskins will be back. He's never been caught yet. I can't help you. It would be too risky with that crazy one out there." She indicated the hall where Jabez was on guard.

The disappointment seemed more than Paula could bear. "You're making a mistake," she said dully.

Mary gave her a sneering glance. "You're not one to threaten. If you don't marry the doctor you'll be our next bit of goods. The medical students will be happy to see a cadaver like you. Give them a treat!" She cackled dryly.

"You'll pay for your crimes, just as Burke did," she told the crone. "Sooner or later you'll make a mistake and be caught. The only decent one among you is Lily."

"Lily!" The old woman wheezed with laughter.

"Yes, Lily," Paula said. "She may be under a curse but she is not pure evil like the rest of you."

The wrinkled face showed a crafty smile. "You're fond of Lily," she said. "Let me show her to you."

She frowned. "What do you mean?"

"Come." The old woman went over to another door and held it open. "Take a look."

Paula advanced cautiously to the door, not certain what to expect. Without crossing the threshold, she peered into the shadows. It was cold and damp in the room and it seemed to have an earthen floor.

"Look over there!" the old woman said, pointing a skinny finger.

She strained to see in the darkness and then the outline of the casket showed itself. A casket on the earthen floor of the room with its top open. There was a body in it.

"Don't you recognize your friend?" the old woman queried artfully.

Consternation crossed Paula's face. The body laid out there could well be Lily. She remembered the woman saying she slept in a coffin by day.

"What is she doing there?" she asked in an awed voice.

"That's where vampires sleep in daylight," the old woman exulted. "In their coffins."

"It can't be!" she said, staring at the form in the coffin in the dark, dank room.

"But it is. Don't count too much on your friend Lily." She shut the door.

Paula stared at the crone. "How long has she been doing this?"

"For more than a hundred years. I was just a girl when I first met her. Lily must be at least a hundred and fifty years old. She's one of the living dead. As long as she gets her supply of blood she'll live on. She got it from you last night."

"It doesn't matter," Paula said, turning away.

"It might," the crone taunted her. "If she bites your throat in the light of the full moon and drains off all your blood instead of just part of it, you'll become a vampire like her!"

"No!"

"It's true!" One Eye Mary insisted. "So that's your fine Lily!"

Paula gave the old woman a sharp glance. "You're making this up to terrify me more. I refuse to believe in vampires."

"Then why does she sleep in a coffin?"

"It may be her only bed," she said, but she knew this was ridiculous. She was beyond her depth and knowledge.

"It is that," the crone said slyly. "Be careful it doesn't become yours."

Paula left the old woman and went back to sit on the cot. The hours went by very slowly. And still there was no sign of Samuel Hoskins. She told herself it had to be a good omen—but it could mean nothing more than that he was in a drunken daze in some tavern, unable to make his way home.

At last dusk came. One Eye Mary was in a state for lack of drink. She had begun to pace restlessly up and down and talk to herself in an unintelligible mumble which Paula couldn't understand. There had been some bread and water in the room and Paula had eaten most of it. It was moldy and vile, but better than nothing.

As dusk came and the light entering the room from its one high barred window dwindled, Mary found a candle and lit it. She set it on the table and went back to her pacing.

Paula was standing below the barred window when she noticed the door of the room in which she'd seen the coffin slowly open. It made her hold her breath. Then from the shadows Lily gradually emerged, looking less calm than when Paula had last seen her. The need for fresh blood was written on her painted, bony face.

"You're still here," she said in a dull voice.

"Yes," Paula said, drawing back.

Lily came further into the room. "I have been sleeping," she said.

"I know."

Lily's burning eyes were fixed on her. "Bentley didn't take you with him?"

"No?"

"Where's Hoskins?"

"He left last night and hasn't come back," she said.

Lily looked across the shadowed room at the old woman pacing and mumbling. "I can see Mary is in a bad upset."

"He was to bring her gin."

Lily nodded. "We all must have our elixirs or we perish." There was a double meaning in her words that sent a chill through Paula.

Lily advanced several more steps across the shadowed room. The painted, bony face had a look of sheer desperation as she stretched out a hand to Paula, who shrank away.

"Wait!" Lily begged. "My thirst is not great!"

"No!" Paula cried, backing away.

"I could make you a bride suitable for Barnabas Collins," Lily said with a wild eagerness. As she reached out for Paula again, there was death in her burning eyes!

CHAPTER 5

"Please, don't!" Paula begged her as she stumbled back.

Lily grasped her arm and drew her close to her. Paula was trapped. She stood frozen as Lily bent toward her neck... Then the door from the hallway burst open and Sam Hoskins came breathlessly into the room.

"The coppers!" he shouted. "They're after me! Coming down the lane!"

Lily swung around with obvious alarm. "Will they get here?"

"Bound to," Hoskins wailed. "They saw me dodge through the arch."

He glared at Paula. "We have to get rid of you, me fine lady!"

"Just let me go free!" she pleaded.

"Likely we will!"

And as Jabez came into the room, he shouted at him, "Get her and put her in Lily's coffin!"

"No!" Paula cried.

In the next instant she was seized by the brown giant and whisked into the room with the earthen floor. Jabez showed no emotion as he thrust her in the coffin and slammed the lid down.

Paula screamed as she found herself a prisoner in the blackness of the closed coffin. She pounded her fists against its cover in an attempt to free herself, but to no avail.

She could hear nothing, could see nothing in the casket. It was as if she were actually entombed. Suddenly she realized that in a short time she would exhaust the small supply of air in the wooden box. Then she would choke to death, horribly and slowly.

This realization made her cry out again and hit the cover in an attempt to burst it open. Already she was finding it difficult to breathe; she began to fear she might lose consciousness. She halted her efforts and forced herself to lie back, exhausted and terrified.

She was as much cut off from the world of the living as if she were actually dead. Hoskins had played his game well. The police would come and search the place and probably never find her. And if Hoskins and the others were sufficiently scared they might not return for days. In the meantime she would die in Lily's coffin.

She speculated on whether her father was with the police. Perhaps Barnabas and John were also along. But she would never see them again. Tears streaked down her cheeks as she waited there in the pitch blackness for death.

And then she heard a scraping and she was conscious of someone working on the cover of the coffin! Her heart gave a great leap! Perhaps help would not come too late after all. The jarring movement came again and suddenly the cover was heaved up and she found herself gazing up at the concerned face of Barnabas.

"Paula!" he said with emotion.

"Barnabas!" She could only manage a tired whisper.

"I knew you must be here somewhere if those villains hadn't murdered you," he said, gently assisting her from the coffin. "Your father and John are searching through the rest of the building with the police."

She looked at his handsome, gaunt face. "How did you know where I was?"

His arm was around her. "Lily," he said. "I came upon her in one of the alleys. She lingered long enough to whisper where they'd hidden you and then fled before the police could catch her."

"What about Hoskins and Jabez and the old woman?"

"They've got One Eye Mary," Barnabas said, still supporting her with his arm. "Hoskins and Jabez got away. That brute Jabez held off the police for minutes and then strangled one before he fled."

"He's some kind of mindless monster," she said.

"I realize that," he said grimly as he helped her out into the larger room.

A candle still flickered on the board table. Even this tiny amount of light was welcome after her ordeal in the blackness of the casket. She could hear the excited voices of the others as they searched through the old house.

She said, "I thought they'd kill me."

"Why did you come down here?"

"Hoskins brought me a note. It was supposed to be from you."

Anger shadowed Barnabas' handsome face. "So that's how they managed it. They used me as the bait."

"I never would have come otherwise," she said. "As soon as I reached here they took me prisoner."

"They didn't harm you?"

"Not beyond terrifying me and shoving me around," she said. "And there was Lily, of course."

Barnabas heard this with a strange expression. "We'll not talk about her."

"It was Dr. Bentley," she said. "He was the one behind it. He came here to see me and tried to make me promise to marry him."

"That scoundrel!"

"I told him how I felt about him and he threatened to have me killed," she said.

"This will not be the end of the affair," Barnabas promised. "Your father will likely raid Dr. Bentley's place."

She shuddered. "He is evil and cruel."

"We know that too well," Barnabas said.

Then her father and John Williams came into the room along with some policemen. Seeing her, Sir Phillip let out a cry of relief and seized her in his arms.

"My child!" he cried, embracing her, with some of the haggardness draining from his aristocratic face. She pressed close to him, thinking of all the terrors she'd endured and how she'd despaired of being with him again.

Now John Williams stepped forward and took one of her hands in his. His square, manly face was lined with worry. "You don't know what we've gone through since you vanished."

She offered him a grateful look. "John, I counted on you being among my rescuers."

"Indeed, he and Barnabas were the leaders," Sir Phillip said with a wan smile for them. "I was too much stricken to take any sensible steps in finding you."

Williams turned to Barnabas. "It was Barnabas who dragged the information about your visitor and 24 Cannon Lane from Ebbets. Your butler had forgotten all about it until Barnabas kept questioning him."

Barnabas, imposing in his caped coat, looked gravely at her father. "I think we should get Paula out of these surroundings at once."

"Quite right," Sir Phillip said, and with his arm around Paula he began assisting her to the door. The police stood back respectfully to let them pass. Barnabas remained behind to speak with the police captain.

They went long the dark alley and through the arch to the other mean street where there were carriages waiting. Sir Phillip helped Paula into one of them and then got in beside her.

"What about Barnabas and John?" she asked.

"They'll come along after conferring with the police," he said. "We'll go directly to Widenham Square and they'll join us there."

She leaned against her father's shoulder. "Widenham Square," she said reverently. "What a world apart it is from this place."

"You must forget this experience," her father advised as the carriage began moving over the cobblestones.

Paula was greeted at the mansion in Widenham Square like a princess returned. There were tears of joy from the housekeeper, Ebbets stammered an apology for his stupidity in not remembering the address sooner and Jane Williams was there to escort her up to her room and stay with her as she washed and changed her clothing after her ordeal.

Her dress was so dirty she gave it to Emma to have burned. And as she luxuriated in a tub of hot water set out in her dressing room, Jane stayed with her, seating herself on a stool.

Paula scrubbed herself and lathered freely with the soap as Emma came running in with another pitcher of hot water. She hovered over the tub anxiously. "Shall I add some more hot, miss?"

Paula, her hair tied in a knot on the top of her head to be free of the water, smiled at her maid and nodded. "Please do add all of it," she said. "This tub is getting cooled off."

"Mind your legs, miss," the maid warned as she poised the pitcher. Paula drew back her shapely legs and Emma poured in the scalding water to mingle with the other.

Paula sighed and mixed the water with her hands and stretched her legs out again. "Heavenly!" she murmured.

Jane gazed at her anxiously. "You're sure you weren't harmed in any way?"

"No, really," she said. "I was dreadfully frightened, but not injured... I saw things I shall never forget."

Jane's eyes narrowed. "There's a small red scar on your neck. It looks like a bite!"

Paula paused in her ablutions, recalling that weird instant when Lily had sunk her fangs in her throat. But Lily had told Barnabas where to find her... "It's nothing. Just a chafe. That giant Jabez was strong and he handled me roughly."

Jane was wide-eyed. "You're so calm about it all," she marveled. "I know I should never have lived through it!"

Paula smiled at her from the tin tub. "Of course you would have! You would have endured for John's sake."

Jane's young face fell. "John was half beside himself after he learned what had happened to you," she said. "I have never seen him so upset."

She blushed. "He worries far too much about me. He is like a brother."

"Yes," Jane said quietly, "like a brother." But she said it in such a way that Paula was afraid she was being more tactful than truthful.

"Bring me my towel, Emma," Paula called out. And she told Jane, "I do want to go downstairs for a moment and thank them all again." She stepped out of the tub as Emma wrapped a large towel around her shapely figure and began to help dry her.

The door to the bedroom burst suddenly open; both Paula and Jane shrieked. Emma moved to close the entrance to the dressing room and hide her mistress from the intruder. But there was no doing this—the intruder was Aunt Lucy, who marched into the dressing room with indignation written on her horsey face.

"Why wasn't I told you'd been found?" she demanded.

"I don't know," Paula said. Tightening the towel around her, she went over and dutifully kissed her aunt.

"I was next door visiting the Tracy Hendersons and had no idea you'd returned until the maid came in and whispered the news to Prunella! I found out about your rescue from someone else's maid," Aunt Lucy fumed. "You can see how important a place I hold in this house!"

"That's not true," Paula said. "I love you dearly. And I'm glad you were over there visiting instead of being here alone worrying."

"I worried just the same," Aunt Lucy assured her. "Are you all right, child?"

"I feel extravagantly good just being here and a little weary," she said.

"You should be in your bed," Aunt Lucy said sternly.

"No," Paula told her as she finished toweling, "I'm going to slip on my kimono and go downstairs and thank father and the others. Then I'll go to bed."

Aunt Lucy turned to Jane and demanded, "Was there ever such a stubborn child as this?"

Jane smiled. "I think Paula is right. They do want to see her a moment. And she looks so much better now."

"Well, I'm sure I have nothing to say about it," Aunt Lucy exclaimed with disgust. "No one in this house listens to me." And she marched out of the room.

Paula went down the great curved stairway a few minutes later with Jane at her side. She was looking her old beautiful self again in a gold kimono with rich brocade trim. As she took in the grandeur of this mansion in which she lived, the place she had just escaped from seemed more like a nightmare than ever.

In her visits to the poor when she was doing her charity work she had seen homes of poverty. But she had been spared the dark and furtive dives of degeneracy, drink and the utterly evil which she'd found in Cannon Lane. She had not guessed such places and people existed.

As she reached the bottom of the stairway Barnabas came forward to take her hand and touch it to his cold lips. "You look ravishing," he said.

Behind him John Williams was smiling. "Much too pretty," he added his compliment.

Her father and Aunt Lucy stood in the background, content that she had been returned to them safely. At the sight of all the beaming, loving faces, her eyes blurred with tears. It was too wonderful to be restored to them!

Barnabas was smiling down at her. "Surely you're not sad about your homecoming?"

"A female's foolish tears," she laughed.

"You're tired," he said. "And now that you have let us see how well you are, I say you should go back to your bedroom at once. You badly need rest."

Her father stepped forward. "Barnabas has given you excellent advice."

"Very well." She smiled. "I'll go on the condition that you'll all come to dinner here tomorrow night. I want to be with you."

"Agreed!" John Williams said heartily, and then looked somewhat embarrassed. He turned to Jane who was standing a little away from him. "We can arrange to come, can't we, Jane?"

She showed a wan smile. "Surely."

"Then it is settled," Barnabas spoke up, covering the awkward situation quickly. "For I shall certainly be here."

"You are all most welcome," Sir Phillip said happily. Paula, escorted by Aunt Lucy, went straight up to bed.

She slept right through the night and most of the following day. It was after four o'clock when she awoke to have some food and take a bath. And she did not make her appearance downstairs until six-thirty when she went down to join her guests.

Barnabas and John Williams were there but Jane had complained of a headache and had not been able to come. Sir Phillip was serving drinks to the small company before going into the dining room. The butler poured a sherry for Paula as she took her place in the circle. They were discussing Dr. Nicholas Bentley.

Sir Phillip was saying, "They raided his house last night and found a partially dissected body which had been stolen from St. Stephen's Cemetery the night before. He was nowhere to be found, nor was his servant Jabez there. The other servants were a poor confused lot who could offer the police no information."

John Williams said, "So he has gone underground. Do you think he will leave London?"

"That is hard to say." Sir Phillip frowned. "But from what I gather, he has embarked on a series of macabre experiments and he is not likely to abandon them."

The young doctor's square face showed disgust. "At least he's finished at the hospital. And I don't see how he can continue a practice in London."

"He can't," Sir Phillip said. "The moment he shows himself he will be arrested for abducting Paula."

Barnabas gave them a look of warning. "I must say that I think there is still danger for all of you, especially Paula and Sir Phillip. If Dr. Bentley is forced to work under cover, he will become more criminal than ever in his activities. He will also blame you people for losing him his practice and his reputation as a doctor. As a martyr, which is how he'll think of himself, he'll be more vicious than before."

Paula listened to this long oration from Barnabas with a growing fear. "Barnabas is right," she said in a hushed voice. "I think the man is mad. And he hates father and John. There is no telling what he may try to do."

Barnabas asked her father, "Have they located Hoskins or Jabez yet?"

"No," Sir Phillip sighed, and finished his sherry. "The police are not too hopeful about catching them, though they have not given up the pursuit. These villains are like rats. They'll burrow deep in the underworld of the city."

John turned to Paula with a smile. "Let us be thankful that we managed to rescue Paula."

"I drink to that," Barnabas said. "And to her continued safety, and that of all of you."

When the toast was over they went into the dining room and the candlelit table. Paula felt she had never tasted such a meal, though it was simple by the measure of some that had been served in the great mansion. But her experience in the slums had taught her to be grateful for even modest pleasures.

Aunt Lucy sat at one end of the table; Sir Phillip presided at the other. Aunt Lucy was full of theories about where Bentley might have vanished.

"I say he has gone to Australia," she insisted. "That is where they are sending all the convicts."

"But he is not a convict," Paula pointed out.

"Just the same, he should be banished to Botany Bay," her aunt said firmly.

When dinner was over Paula unexpectedly found herself in the company of John Williams. The others had drifted to a different part of the drawing room. The young physician seemed ill at ease, now that they were alone.

Suddenly he told her, "Jane doesn't really have a headache tonight."

"Doesn't she?"

"No," he said with a shadow on his square face. "She refused to come. She felt it was paying you too much tribute. She's jealous of you, you must know that. She thinks I'm still in love with you!"

"But she should know better," Paula protested.

His eyes met hers solemnly. "I'm sorry, Paula, but it happens to be true. I do still love you."

Her cheeks warmed. She looked away. "I don't want to hear that, John. You didn't say it."

"I said it," he replied in a troubled voice. "And I'm not sorry that I did."

Barnabas came over to them and she at once turned her back on John, aware that her cheeks were still flaming and feeling guilty that she should be causing unhappiness in the marriage of two friends.

Barnabas smiled at her. "You're blushing. Did you know?"

"It's warm in here," she said.

"And too cold to step out on the balcony," Barnabas said. "Could we try another room?"

Eager to get away from John Williams for a while, she said, "Yes. Let us do that. I'm sure no one will be annoyed if we slip across to the library for a little."

Barnabas escorted her across the foyer to the library where candles burned on the mantel and on several of the tables. It was a large gracious room. She seated herself in an easy chair and held her fan up to her bosom as Barnabas stood facing her.

With a wry smile, Barnabas said, "I must say no one has reproved you for running off the way you did. I hope you'll not embark on another such adventure again."

"I have learned my lesson," she promised.

"You were warned not to leave the house, or even the square, alone, and yet you did."

"I thought the message was from you," she reminded him.

Barnabas smiled. "I'm pleased that my name had such urgency for you. But even if you should receive such a message again, you mustn't do anything about it."

"I promise."

"I think the danger is far from over," he warned her. "I can't impress that on you too much."

"I believe you," she said very seriously. "I was touched that close by the evil."

"London has grown to be too large a city," Barnabas said. "And we have an underworld of criminals which threatens its very existence."

She gave him a questioning look. "What about Lily?"

He frowned. "What about her?"

"According to you, she saved my life."

"Well?"

"Isn't there something we can do for her?" Paula worried. "Some way we can help her? She's very ill. I hate to think of her wandering out in the dark streets at night."

Barnabas was regarding her with a strange expression on his handsome face. "Did she tell you the nature of her illness?"

"She drank my blood," Paula said simply. "I didn't know there were humans suffering from such a dreadful curse."

"Well, you know now," Barnabas said with a deep sigh.

"Can she be helped?"

He shrugged. "There have been experiments. Some have worked for a while. But invariably the afflicted person returns to his old state. You mustn't think about Lily. She has roamed the streets for years and there's no reason to worry about her. There are many more like her, you know."

She got to her feet, facing him solemnly. "I didn't know. Not until I met her." She paused, her eyes meeting his deep-set ones. "She told me that you share the same curse, Barnabas."

He looked more gaunt than ever, and more noble. Quietly, he said, "What do you want me to say?"

"Tell me the truth, Barnabas. Is that why you are seen only at night? Why no one can reach you during the days?"

Barnabas hesitated a moment before he nodded. "Yes."

The candlelight was playing on his handsome face. She gazed at him with gentle eyes. "My poor Barnabas!" she said softly. "Why didn't you tell me before? Were you afraid it would make a difference with me?"

"It is a painful subject I prefer not to discuss," he said quietly.

Paula moved close to him. "I'm in love with you, Barnabas. You must have guessed that long ago. And I worried that you didn't love me. I couldn't understand why you held back telling me that you cared. Now I understand."

Barnabas was frowning. "If I loved you," he said carefully, "I would not feel privileged to tell you until I had found a cure for my vampirism."

"But that's nonsense," she protested. "If you suffered from any other illness and still loved me I would understand. I want to be your wife. I'll stand by you until you are restored to a normal existence again. There must be a cure."

His hands were on her arms and he was staring down at her earnestly. "That is a sacrifice I'm not prepared to have you make," he said. "I shall always be your friend. And if I'm fortunate enough to rid myself of this cursed condition before you marry another, I shall surely bid for your hand. That is all we can hope for."

"Barnabas!" she murmured brokenly.

He held her close in his arms and kissed her. They were still locked in an embrace when John Williams came into the room. He halted quickly and said, "Sorry!"

Paula drew away from Barnabas. "It's all right. We don't mind. You know that Barnabas and I will soon be announcing our engagement."

John looked upset. "No, I didn't know that," he said stiffly. And he offered his hand to Barnabas. "Congratulations."

Barnabas took his hand. "I'm afraid Paula's announcement was somewhat premature," he told him. "I would appreciate it if you would consider it a secret."

"You may depend on me, both of you," Williams said with his pleasant face still showing his distress. "If you'll excuse me." He turned and quickly left them alone in the library.

Barnabas gave her a reproachful glance. "Why did you tell him that?"

"Because I hope it will be true," she said. "And because he thinks himself still in love with me and I want to discourage him. Jane is my good friend."

Barnabas smiled tolerantly. "I can forgive you for the latter reason. But never embarrass me by coming out with such a statement again."

Paula looked up at him lovingly. "Oh, Barnabas, I do care for you so much."

"You should find yourself a younger, healthy suitor," Barnabas said. "I can't expect you to wait for me."

"But I will," she said. "I promise you I will."

"It is time we joined the others," Barnabas said wryly. And he led her back to the drawing room.

The evening passed quickly. Paula played some selections on the pianoforte and for a little the dreadful experiences she'd gone through in the slimy darkness of Cannon Lane were forgotten. But when she stopped playing she remembered. And she knew she would always remember. The horror was etched on her mind.

She and her father said goodnight to Barnabas, who left looking more heartbreakingly handsome than ever in his flowing dark cape. And then Dr. John Williams offered his goodnights.

Paula told him, "Be sure and tell Jane I was inquiring for her. And that I trust her headache will soon be better."

"I will," he said, his square face going crimson. "Goodnight, Paula."

Her father saw him to the door.

With the last of their company gone, they went upstairs to bed. Paula kissed her father and Aunt Lucy goodnight and went on to her own room. Emma already had the bed turned down and greeted her with a curtsy and a smile.

"Did you have a pleasant evening, miss?" she asked.

Paula eyed her archly. "I hope you weren't peeking at us from the parlor back door again," she said. "Or you may have seen me in someone's arms."

"Oh, la, miss!" the girl giggled. "I wouldn't dare mention it if I had."

She smiled at the girl and crossed to the window. Parting the drapes, she gazed out to see if there was a promise of rain. And then her eyes wandered to the square and she gasped. For there, staring up at her window with strange, unseeing eyes, was the monstrous Jabez!

CHAPTER 6

Quickly letting the drape fall back into place, she rushed out of her bedroom and ran down the hall to her father's room and knocked frantically on the door. "Father, it's Paula!" she cried.

The door was opened almost immediately and her father, in dressing gown, came out to her. "What is it?"

"Jabez," she said breathlessly. "I saw him just now standing in the square outside my window."

"Bentley's servant?"

"Yes."

"Show me," Sir Phillip said, his aristocratic face taut with concern as they hurried down the corridor to her room again.

Emma was standing to one side, looking frightened, when they entered the bedroom. Paula took her father directly to the window and pulled back the drapes for him to see. But Jabez had vanished!

She frowned as she stared down into the dark square. "He's gone!"

"You're sure he was there?" her father asked. "It wasn't just a case of nerves on your part?"

"No!"

"Very well," he said. "I accept your word."

She turned to him with troubled eyes. "I saw him. There's no mistaking that monster! He must have left while I was on my way to get you."

Her father sighed. "Since he isn't there now, I'm afraid there's little we can do."

"He'll come back again," she predicted. "He could still be down there in the shadows hiding."

"Without a doubt," her father said, his patrician face serious. "Why not have Emma remain in your room for the night, just as a safeguard? She'll be company in case you are bothered again."

She hesitated. "I don't know."

"I think you should do that. There's a cot in the dressing room she can use. I'll feel less worried." He turned to the maid. "You don't mind using the cot, do you, Emma?"

Emma shook her head. "No. I'd be glad to stay here with Miss Paula."

"Then it's settled," Sir Phillip said. To Paula, he promised, "I'll visit the police station in the morning and explain that we are being bothered again."

"I hope they soon arrest Jabez and the others," Paula said, tension showing on her pretty face.

"I think they'll get them," her father said. "They usually do."

After he returned to his own room, Emma made herself a bed on the cot and they all settled down for the night. But Paula did not sleep at once. She kept seeing that cruel brown face with the weird, blank eyes staring up from the shadows. The terror was by no means over yet.

The next day it rained. And in the late afternoon Prunella Henderson, excited and talkative, came to have afternoon tea with Paula and Aunt Lucy.

"Did you see that huge, weird man loitering in the square last night?" was almost the first question she asked as they sat around a table in the rear parlor.

Paula nodded. "Yes. It's the one called Jabez. The police are looking for him."

"Then he is one of that gang who abducted you!" Prunella gasped. "I thought he must be!"

"He should be in prison this very minute!" Aunt Lucy said grimly.

"He is utterly mad," Paula said quietly. "The very sight of him is terrifying."

Prunella's pretty face was forlorn. "We are all in danger as long as he is around."

"I think his evil is directed mostly toward my father and me," she said quietly. "He works for Dr. Nicholas Bentley and does whatever he tells him."

"Dr. Bentley ran off and left his practice, didn't he?" Prunella said.

"The blackguard!" Aunt Lucy snapped.

"They say he led a Black Magic Circle," Prunella said, her eyes sparkling with excitement. "I hear they did all kinds of monstrous things. The meetings were held in his house, they say, and some of the most prominent men and beautiful women of the town were drawn into his wicked group."

Paula said, "No doubt some of it is exaggerated."

"There has to be some truth behind it," Prunella argued. "Stories like that don't get repeated unless there's something."

"I grant you that."

Her friend's eyes were wide. "They say the masses were exactly like Christian ones in reverse. That Bentley and his followers worshiped the Devil."

"He is an evil man," Paula said.

"You should know better than anyone else," Prunella said. "And I heard that the purpose of his Black Magic meetings was to restore the dead to life. Imagine that!" She poised her teacup daintily, looking horrified.

Paula was thinking of all the things she'd discovered while a prisoner in the slums, and of what she had learned about Barnabas, the man she loved. She said, "There are many strange things going on in London."

"Satan himself has taken over," was Aunt Lucy's opinion.

Prunella leaned forward to Paula eagerly. "I'm sure you must have seen some horrible things when they were holding you in that slum."

The frivolous desire for sensation distressed Paula. "I am trying to forget what I saw and endured."

Prunella looked disappointed. "Of course," she said coolly. "You are right in that."

Paula sat alone in her bedroom for a long while after her visitor had gone home. Forgetting was not going to be as easy as she'd hoped; the horror of her experiences still haunted her. And she shuddered as she realized how easy it would be to be caught up in the same terrors again.

Dinner was a quiet affair that evening. Her father seemed strangely silent and occupied with thoughts which he kept to himself. Aunt Lucy was glum and Paula had not the energy to keep conversation going at the table. When the meal was over, Aunt Lucy went upstairs and Paula and Sir Phillip went to the drawing room for a talk.

"I spoke to the police this morning," her father said. "But they've had no word of where Bentley is. Though they seem to think they've got information on Sam Hoskins that could lead to his capture."

"Let us hope so," she said fervently.

"The police have also promised to keep a close watch on the square and this house in particular," her father said worriedly. "And that's about all that can be done."

"I suppose so."

He gave her a sharp glance. "You must be more cautious than ever. Don't leave the house without an escort."

"I've learned my lesson," she promised him.

"One would hope so. Until those villains are caught, it is a matter of waiting and being patient."

They went on talking quietly until they were interrupted by the sound of excited voices in the hallway. And then Ebbets showed in a highly agitated elderly man.

Ebbets appeared almost flustered as he told them, "This is Peters, Dr. John Williams' manservant. He has some information for you, he says."

"Indeed I have, Sir Phillip and Miss Sullivan," Peters explained excitedly. "I have the most dreadful news. My master and mistress were attacked and kidnapped from the house about an hour ago!"

Paula felt weak and ill. "No!"

Her father quickly placed an arm around her. His face was ashen as he demanded, "Go on, Peters. Tell me all the details."

The old man twisted his hat in his hands. "There isn't much I can tell you, sir. I was in the kitchen when it happened. They somehow got into the house and upstairs where my master and mistress were. If one of the maids hadn't happened to see the villains dragging out Dr. John and his wife we wouldn't have known what to think."

"Were John and his wife alive at this point? Offering any resistance?" Sir Phillip demanded.

"Not according to the maid. She claimed they were both unconscious and maybe dead. There was a big brown man and a small stooped one. The brown man was carrying Mr. John and the little man had the mistress."

"Bentley's thugs," her father said. "Perhaps Bentley will use their bodies for his experiments. This is how he settled his account with poor John and Jane."

Paula pleaded with her parent, "Can't we do something to help them?"

"We can try, assuming they are not beyond help," her father said grimly. He asked the old servant, "Have you told the police of this?"

Peters nodded. "Yes. I sent a footman to the station. And I'm going back there now. The police should have arrived."

Sir Phillip frowned. "No doubt," he said. "I'll go over at once. I can talk to the police and perhaps be of some help."

Peters said, "Thank you, Sir Phillip. I knew Dr. John would want you informed. I'll see you back at the house." And he went out with Ebbets at his side.

Sir Phillip turned to Paula, "I must go over there at once."

"Take me along," she said.

He hesitated. "I think not."

"I want to go," she insisted. "You must allow me to accompany you. It is possible I may be of some use."

Her father considered this. "Very well," he finally said. "Put on your things and be ready to leave in ten minutes."

So within a very short space of time she was seated with her father in their carriage as it rolled across the cobble-stoned streets of London. The gas lamps on the dark street corners showed a welcome orange glow and occasionally revealed a uniformed policeman strolling along.

Staring out the carriage window into the darkness of the city Paula contemplated what a jungle it was when daylight ended. Even here in the better residential district there were bizarre crimes taking place in great mansions with a facade of respectability. How easy it had been for Jabez and Hoskins to enter the Williams home, overpower Jane and John, and take them prisoner!

At last the carriage came to a halt before a modest two-story brick house with white columns at either side of its door. They left the carriage and walked up the steps where they were accosted by a burly police officer.

"What's your business here?" the officer wanted to know.

"I'm Sir Phillip Sullivan, a colleague of Dr. Williams," her father said. "And this is my daughter. We've come as friends and to offer any help we can about the nature of the crime."

"You can go in, Sir Phillip," the officer said. "The sergeant is expecting you."

Sergeant Snell, a grizzled veteran of the department, seemed well acquainted with the background of the crime. He found chairs for Sir Phillip and Paula in the living room of the Williams' house and then stood politely as he asked a number of questions.

"It would appear, Sir Phillip, that this kidnapping and possible double murder has a direct connection with the resurrectionists," the sergeant said.

Her father nodded. "Yes. And of course Dr. Nicholas Bentley is the evil brain behind it all."

Sergeant Snell looked cynical. "That's something we have yet to prove," he pointed out. "But we do know that this Bentley was buying bodies dug up from graveyards, and some murdered by thugs. A strictly illegal traffic, which you and this young Dr. Williams opposed."

"Definitely," her father said. "That is why this has happened. And why they abducted my daughter."

The grizzled sergeant turned his attention to her. "You were kept a prisoner by them," he said. "So no doubt you would be able to identify any of the lot?"

"Yes. Easily," she said quietly.

"We have a tip on Hoskins," the sergeant said. "We hope to bring him in. Possibly he'll lead us to the others."

"I trust so," Sir Phillip said. "And I pray that John and his wife are in no danger of being murdered. This is a most damnable business!"

"Yes, sir," Sergeant Snell agreed.

They remained at the Williams house for hours. Paula rested in a big chair, feeling sick with fear and dreadfully weary. Meanwhile her father gave his full cooperation to the police. It was close to midnight when she heard a voice from the hall that made her sit bolt upright and then she rose and hurried out to the dimly lighted hallway to see a haggard John Williams, supported by a police man. Her father and the sergeant were facing him.

Her father exclaimed, "Thank heavens you're safe, John! Where is Jane?"

John's eyes were glazed. "They kept her."

Sergeant Snell frowned. "You mean to say they let you go and kept her a prisoner?"

John nodded miserably. His face was dirty and his clothes dishevelled and torn. "It was meant as an extra torment for me."

Paula went toward him. "Dear John!"

He gave her a piteous glance. "Paula!"

Her father said, "He must be attended to and put to bed at once. You bring him upstairs. Sergeant, and I'll look after him medically."

She stood by as the sergeant and the other officer helped John up the stairs, with her father leading the way. She was shocked by John's shattered condition, and she could imagine the torture he was going through knowing that poor Jane was at the mercy of the resurrectionists. She waited in the drawing room for the better part of an hour before her father came downstairs.

"He's in a bad state," her father worried. "Much of it is mental. But they were physically cruel to him as well. His chief concern now is what may have happened to his wife."

"Poor Jane!" she mourned.

"I know." Her father frowned. "There is nothing we can do here now. I'll take you back to Widenham Square."

It wasn't until noon the next day that Jane's fate was known. Her body turned up mysteriously in the medical school of Winslow Hospital. Someone had spirited it in there during the night and when Sir Phillip removed the sheet from a cadaver on a marble slab in the morgue he was confronted by Jane's nude body.

That night Barnabas Collins was a visitor at the great mansion of Sir Phillip Sullivan in Widenham Square. He, Sir Phillip, and Paula discussed this latest horror before the fireplace in the drawing room.

Sir Phillip said, "I took it upon myself to acquaint poor John with the fate of his dear wife. Fortunately he is still in a state of shock and so his reaction to the news was not as violent as I'd expected. He seemed rather more dazed. But to be on the safe side I sedated him with some tincture of opium."

Barnabas said grimly, "Bentley should be caught and hung."

"I couldn't agree more," Paula said with sorrowful anger.

"I am sure the police are doing everything they can," Sir Phillip said.

"I would like to see the case finished," Barnabas said. "I plan to return to America shortly. I'm going back to my birthplace of Collinsport for a visit. And I would like to feel Paula was out of danger before I leave."

Her father nodded. "I understand. And we appreciate the interest you have taken in all this."

The handsome face of Barnabas was sad. "I wish I had been able to do more. Jane Williams was a lovely young woman. I hate to think of her the victim of those murderers."

Sir Phillip said, "A high price for John to pay for his fight against the grave robbers. I doubt if he will ever be fully himself again. An experience such as this could mark a man for life."

Paula looked up at her father anxiously, "Do you feel he'll have to give up doctoring?"

"Perhaps not, but there is a chance of it. He will always be haunted by this tragedy."

Later, when she was seeing Barnabas to the door and her father had left them alone, Barnabas paused in the shadows, to tell her, "It may be that you will play the role of John's angel of mercy."

Surprise showed in her lovely brown eyes. "What do you mean?"

"He is a widower now."

"Well?"

Barnabas said solemnly, "He is in sore distress. He needs someone to be close to him, to encourage him to begin life afresh."

"I shall certainly be a friend to him."

"Why not his wife?" The question was startlingly blunt.

She gasped. "But I love you."

"We know that isn't possible as things are," he said, his handsome face set in grim lines.

"It will be one day."

"You could marry John soon and help him build a second life and marriage."

"No," she said. "Never."

"You should think it over."

"You know such talk is useless," she chided him. "Kiss me goodnight, Barnabas."

He smiled gently. "What a stubborn creature you are!" But he took her in his arms and gave her a tender kiss.

She stood in the doorway as he walked down the steps and across the foggy cobblestoned street. As she watched she thought she saw a figure move furtively away to the left in the mist. But a second glance disclosed no one and so she decided she had been wrong. With a sigh she closed and locked the door and went upstairs to her bedroom.

Emma was waiting for her. "Another foggy night, miss."

"It is," she said as she removed her necklace.

"Cook said it was the proper kind of night for a killing," Emma went on, her small face pinched with anxiety.

"Cook talks too much and too loosely."

She was about to sit before her dresser when she heard the scuffle of running footsteps from the corridor outside. She turned around with fear on her face and then came a high-pitched shriek from her father. She ran to the door with Emma following her, grabbing at her arm.

"Don't go out there, miss!"

Paula pushed her aside. "My father is in danger!"

In the next instant she was in the shadowed corridor and saw her father struggling in Jabez's grasp as the monster dragged him towards the circular stairway.

"Let him go!" she screamed, and raced along the hall to the giant and began pounding on his back. Jabez didn't pay the slightest attention to her.

"Let my father free!" Paula screamed again.

As she watched in horror, the sleepwalking giant lifted her father's slim body high above his head and hurled him down the winding, steep stairway as hard as he could. Paula gripped the railing as she saw her father crash down on the stairway, roll, and sprawl motionless at the bottom.

Crouching, she accused Jabez, "You've killed him! You've killed my father!"

The blank face before her still showed no expression. He turned and lumbered off down the other hallway and vanished in the dark. She ran down the stairs to her father's broken body and cradled his bleeding head in her arms. His eyes were closed; she knew instinctively there was no breath of life left in him.

"Miss Sullivan." The words came slyly from above her and she lifted her eyes in a daze to look up at the dirty, beard-stubbled face of Sam Hoskins standing on the step over her.

"Go away!" she gasped in horror.

"And you'll be coming with me, miss." The toothless gums showed in a menacing smile as he reached down and seized her arm.

"No!" She tried to escape him without success.

He roughly raised her to her feet and with a sneering glance at her father's body, he told her, "You won't do him no good staying here. Dr. Bentley has plans for you."

She clawed her nails down his cheek, bringing blood. But he only laughed and caught her free hand. Then he twisted her other arm so she shrieked with pain as he propelled her forward down the stairway. In the foyer she saw Ebbets sprawled out on the carpet, where Jabez had no doubt left him unconscious or dead. Even in her desperate plight she wondered vaguely about Aunt Lucy.

"Just take it easy, me pretty," Sam Hoskins chuckled as she struggled to free herself. They were almost to the front door now. She had a feeling that if she ever went through it she'd never see Widenham Square again. Hoskins gave her arm another twist and the searing pain made her forget everything else.

He reached out and opened the door—and then fell back in surprise. Barnabas Collins stood framed in the doorway, a look of rage on his handsome face. He had unsheathed the concealed sword in his walking stick and held it on the ready.

Stepping inside, he said, "Drop her!"

Hoskins let her go at once. "No offense, mate!" he said, gazing at the sword with fear-stricken eyes.

Barnabas advanced on him. "You scum!"

"Please!" Hoskins raised his hands for mercy.

But Barnabas was stalking him, cornering him so that he could not make a run for freedom. The filthy, stooped man was babbling wildly and falling over furniture as he edged along the wall trying to shelter himself.

Then the sword flashed like a streak of lightning and found its mark in Hoskins' right arm—the arm which had been used to torture her so. Barnabas drove the blade all the way through the upraised arm, pinning it to the wall and Hoskins with it. Hoskins gave a low moan.

"That takes care of you!" Barnabas said angrily. And then he turned to Paula, who was sitting on the floor. "Are you hurt?" he asked.

"No," she moaned. She pointed to the stairs. "Father!"

Concern shadowed his handsome face. He quickly went to the stairs where her father lay. He was only gone a short time before he returned.

At the same moment Sergeant Snell entered the front door with several of his men. He saw her on the floor and Hoskins still pinned against the wall by the sword.

He told Barnabas, "You did well enough here! We lost the West Indian. He made a break for it across the square. We shot at him but it didn't do any good."

"I wouldn't expect it to," Barnabas replied.

"He's gone anyway," Sergeant Snell said. "But you've got Hoskins. Is the young lady all right?"

"She's safe," Barnabas said. "Her father is dead. Ebbets is

unconscious and I don't know what's happened upstairs."

Paula heard no more... she had fainted. And when she came to, she was in the rear parlor on a divan with Barnabas seated by her.

She looked up at him in pitiful despair. "Barnabas!" she moaned.

"You must have courage," he said. "Your father would expect that in you."

"Aunt Lucy?"

"Safe. They locked her in her room."

"And the others?"

"None of the servants were harmed, except Ebbets. And he's recovering. He was only stunned," Barnabas said.

"Poor father!"

"I know how you feel," Barnabas said gently.

"How did you know?"

"That you were in danger?"

"Yes."

He looked grim. "When I left the house, I spotted Sam Hoskins hiding by some shrubbery in the shadows. I pretended not to have noticed him and continued on my way."

"I thought I saw someone move in the darkness," she recalled.

"It was Hoskins," Barnabas said. "I went on out to the square and found that Sergeant Snell and some of his men had been assigned to watch the district. I told them they should surround the house and see if they could catch the gang."

"They got in before the police arrived," she said. "I heard father cry out."

Barnabas frowned. "I'm sorry Jabez got away. But at least we have Sam Hoskins."

"Maybe he'll tell us where Bentley is hiding."

"I hope so," Barnabas said. "He's out in the kitchen now. The police fixed up his arm and they're questioning him."

She at once sat up. "Let me go out there. I want to hear what he knows."

Barnabas frowned. "Do you feel up to it?"

"I must."

"There's no need. I'll find out for you."

Paula was firm in her demand. She got to her feet. "Take me to him, Barnabas."

He put a supporting arm around her and they started for the kitchen in the rear of the mansion. When they reached it the police were standing around a chair on which a cowering Samuel Hoskins was seated. There was a bandage on his arm and fear written across his ugly face.

He was telling Sergeant Snell, "What Dr. Bentley has is this plan for reviving dead bodies. Just like the witch doctors did to Jabez."

CHAPTER 7

As they entered the shadowed kitchen, Sergeant Snell came forward with a concerned look on his broad face. "Do you think this is any place for the young lady, sir?" he inquired of Barnabas.

Barnabas said, "She wishes to hear what Hoskins has to say. This is her house and she has suffered much at the hands of these villains. I feel she should be allowed to remain."

The sergeant glanced at her worriedly. "Some of the things he's been telling us aren't too pretty."

"I've been through a good deal," she said quietly. "I want to listen to his story."

"Very well," the sergeant said. "You can take her to a chair over there, Mr. Collins."

Barnabas led her over to a plain kitchen chair across the room from the one Hoskins was seated in. The policemen stared at her with undisguised interest.

The sight of Barnabas seemed to be making Hoskins more frightened than ever. His eyes rolled and he kept looking from one policeman to the other. His hairy hands were folded in his lap.

Sergeant Snell came forward to him with a stern look on his broad face. "Now, my man, let us hear more."

Hoskins licked his lips. "Well, as I said, this Dr. Bentley has kind of gone crazy since he had to go in hiding. He isn't satisfied with just any corpse any longer. He keeps telling me that I have to get ones that are still warm."

The sergeant said, "Which you no doubt were prepared to do."

Hoskins was a caricature of injured innocence. "Oh, I wouldn't do anything violent like. The thought never entered me head. But if I knew someone what had an old mum or dad about ready to croak off I'd speak to them and ask them to let me know right soon. That way I could get the bodies warm the way he liked them."

Sergeant Snell said, "Bentley wanted young, strong bodies, not the pathetic wrecks of poor old people. I don't believe your story."

" 'Struth," Sam Hoskins said miserably. "I wouldn't lie to you, your honor. I have respect for the law."

"You displayed that here tonight," the sergeant said. "You're not even a good liar."

Barnabas asked the sergeant, "Would you have him explain why Bentley wanted the bodies warm?"

Snell nodded and turned to Hoskins. "Tell us that, Hoskins. Why did the bodies have to be warm?"

"For what he wanted to do with them," the grave robber said. "He means to bring them back to life."

"Back to life?"

"Something like that," Hoskins said, very uneasy. "You see, he found the witch doctors doing it in the Indies and he bought Jabez from them. Jabez hasn't got any more mind than a stone. But he does everything that Bentley tells him. He's a zombie. One of the living dead who the witch doctors raised from his grave with voodoo."

"Does Bentley practice voodoo?" the sergeant asked.

"Yes." The crafty, beard-stubbled face showed fear. "He believes in voodoo. And he's developed this serum of his own. He told me, 'I'll be the richest man in the world if what I'm doing turns out.' And I asks him what he's doing. And he smiles at me and says, 'Just make sure the bodies are warm and supple when they reach me and you'll be doing your part.' Well, I told him I wasn't sure I wanted any messing around with things like that."

"And?"

Hoskins looked and sounded abject, "He cursed at me the way he always did. And he threatened to have Jabez kill me if I didn't do what he ordered."

"A likely story," the sergeant snapped.

"I swear it," Hoskins whined. Looking at Paula, he said, "You ask her if it ain't so. She must have heard him threaten me. I was scared of my skin most of the time!"

"Just leave the young lady out of it. We are interested in your story."

Samuel Hoskins hunched uncomfortably. "Well, like I said, he threatened me so I would go out looking for bodies warm and supple, like he ordered. I talked to him about it one day and asked what he hoped to do with them. And he said after he'd restored them to the same mindless life as Jabez he would use them. They'd be his slaves. Ready to do anything he told them. And yet they'd look and act normal like to everyone."

The sergeant frowned. "He was planning to unleash an army of mindless dead all over London to murder, steal or commit any kind of crime for him?"

The grave robber nodded. "That's about it."

"Did you ever see him give them this serum? I mean the dead people you brought him."

"No, sir," Hoskins said. "He wouldn't let me watch any of his experiments."

"But you feel he did succeed?"

Hoskins didn't answer for a moment. Then reluctantly he said, "I guess maybe the serum worked. He did revive some of them."

Sergeant Snell turned to Barnabas. "Did you ever hear a more incredible yarn?"

Barnabas looked solemn. "The danger is that it is true. May I question him, Sergeant?"

The grizzled Snell gave him a resigned look. "If you like."

Barnabas moved over to stand before the toothless, dirty Sam Hoskins. "You know I could have as easily killed you tonight as run my sword through your arm?"

Hoskins looked sullen. "Yes, sir."

"I spared your life so you could help the police run down Dr. Bentley and bring an end to his criminal actions. Are you ready to do that?"

"What's it get me?" Hoskins wanted to know.

Sergeant Snell answered him. "If you turn evidence for the Crown I can recommend you for leniency, though I know very well you don't deserve any."

Hoskins sneered at him. "Just so long as I get my rights."

"You will," Barnabas assured him. "Did you ever see a body that you'd brought to Bentley revived?"

"Yes," Hoskins said.

"How many?"

"One or two. I don't rightly remember. When I saw them walking and talking I was too afraid to stay around long."

Barnabas regarded him contemptuously. "You are short on courage, aren't you, Hoskins? Except when it comes to abusing women. Then you suddenly become brave."

"No, sir," Hoskins snapped.

"The most important thing at the moment is Bentley's whereabouts," Barnabas said. "Do you know where he is?"

"No, I don't."

"That doesn't ring true," Barnabas told him. "You were planning to take Miss Sullivan to him this very night."

"Wrong, sir, beggin' your pardon," the grave robber said.

"Explain."

Sam Hoskins hunched again and with an evil glance for Barnabas said, "Why do you ask me all these things? Why don't you question Lily? She's your friend!"

"Let's leave Lily out of this," Barnabas said angrily.

Sergeant Snell gave him a curious glance. "Who's Lily?"

Barnabas shrugged. "A girl of the streets whom I happen to know. She has nothing to do with all this."

"She was always around Bentley," Hoskins spoke up defiantly, anxious to accuse his accuser. "And she's your sort!"

"What sort?" It was Sergeant Snell who put the question sharply to the grave robber.

Paula held her breath. Suddenly she was afraid for Barnabas. Hoskins was ready to reveal him as a vampire like the unfortunate Lily. If he did this, Barnabas would be placed in a bad position with the police. Any unexplained murder was sooner or later charged to a vampire.

Barnabas spoke up before Hoskins could reply. He said, "I think this man is referring to the fact that before Lily fell on evil times she was a member of the theatrical profession. I also am of the theatre, being a playwright. But I make no apologies for the fact."

Satisfied, the sergeant turned to Hoskins. "Mr. Collins is right. The thing we want to know most is where Bentley has his headquarters now."

"I don't know."

"You were meeting him tonight," the sergeant reminded him.

"On the embankment," Hoskins said abjectly. "That's where I've been meeting him lately and turning the bodies over to Jabez, who is always with him. Along the embankment. He hasn't let me know where he's hiding out since the raid on his place."

"Not a very likely story," Sergeant Snell said.

Sam Hoskins shrugged. "I can't help it! I've told you all I know!"

The sergeant looked disgusted. "Take him away," he told the policemen who'd been standing by. "His memory may improve in prison."

Paula watched as the police guided their sullen captive out of the kitchen. He shuffled along in his familiar way, his head bent.

She was positive he'd betray no more information about Dr. Nicholas Bentley. Fear of reprisal would prevent him from talking.

Sergeant Snell came over to her and Barnabas with a frown on his lined face. "I'm afraid we didn't get much from him."

Barnabas sighed. "He's a hardened criminal type. We can't hope for too much."

"Exactly, sir," the Sergeant said respectfully. And he turned to Paula, "It is too bad about your father, Miss Sullivan. He was a fine man. We meant to protect him. Is there anything we can do?"

"No," Paula said dully. She was only now beginning to realize that her father was lost to her for all time.

"You'll have a guard in the house, won't you?" Barnabas asked.

"I'll leave a man here for as long as it seems necessary," the sergeant promised. "Depend on that."

He left them and Barnabas took her upstairs to Aunt Lucy's room. The old woman was prostrate with grief in bed. Barnabas said goodnight and she remained with her aunt.

The days that followed were confused and full of sadness. Barnabas helped her with all the details, but he was not able to attend her father's funeral on a bleak, sunless afternoon two days after the murder. She understood why and had to make excuses for him to Aunt Lucy.

She arranged for Barnabas to join them at dinner one evening about a week after the funeral. She also invited John Williams, but he asked to be excused. He was still in a shattered state over Jane's murder and didn't even look like himself. His cheeks had hollowed and there were dark circles under his eyes. He behaved like an old man. The brief appearance he'd made as a pallbearer for Paula's father had left her shocked at the change in the young doctor.

Barnabas arrived promptly on time for the seven o'clock dinner and afterwards he, Paula and Aunt Lucy sat together in the drawing room, discussing what should be done in the future.

"I say you should leave London," Barnabas recommended. "Probably get right away from England. Dr. Bentley is still at large in the city somewhere, and while he is, you are in dreadful danger."

Aunt Lucy had become feeble from the shock of events and now leaned forward to say, "But didn't Dr. Bentley go to Australia?"

"No, madam," Barnabas said. "I believe it was your conjecture that he might. But we have no proof of it."

The old woman nodded sagely. "All scoundrels are being sent out there by the government."

"Not Bentley," Barnabas said. "I'm positive he is still hidden somewhere here in London conducting his macabre experiments to bring the dead to life."

Paula was pale and quiet, but bitter in her desire for revenge. She said, "I should like to stay here until he is arrested and see him hang!"

Aunt Lucy looked scandalized. "That is most unladylike!"

"Perhaps," Paula said. "But it is how I feel."

Barnabas gave her a warning look. "I think you would be flirting with death to remain here. I advise you at least take an extended holiday until Bentley is arrested." She knew there was much truth in what he said. Yet she was loath to leave London with Bentley unpunished. It made her angry to think that he could still have the power to force her from her fine home in Widenham Square.

She said, "I can't leave Aunt Lucy here alone." Barnabas' handsome face was lined with concern. "I do not feel your aunt is open to the same danger you are. She can easily hire a companion to keep her company until your return."

"Of course I can," Aunt Lucy said with a trace of her former spirit. "I'm still not a helpless old woman, in spite of what you may think."

Paula smiled wanly. "There is no place I particularly want to go. I dislike the idea of spending a long period in a foreign clime with strangers."

The deep-set eyes of Barnabas met hers. "You know that I am leaving London."

A hint of panic came to her. "I hope not," she pleaded. "I need you so much now."

"You have John Williams."

"John is only a shadow of his former self," she said. "It will take a long while before he recovers from his tragedy."

"Why not accompany me to America?" Barnabas suggested. "You can stay at the estate of Collinwood with my cousins, James and Maria Collins. They are rather dour but good people. They would enjoy having a visitor to regale them with tales of London life."

The thought of going to America had never occurred to her. Now it seemed an interesting possibility, especially since it meant she would be remaining close to Barnabas. She said, "Are you serious?"

"Of course," he said. "I'll be living at the old house on the estate, which is only a few minutes walk from Collinwood. I could visit you every evening. There would be no need for you to be lonely and you would be away from the threat of Dr. Nicholas Bentley."

"You make it sound very appealing."

Aunt Lucy spoke up. "Perhaps you should discuss it with John Williams first. You know of his interest in you."

"No," Paula said firmly. "If I mention it to John, I'm sure he'll try to argue against my leaving London. And I think I will." She offered Barnabas a forlorn smile. "Aren't you worried about being burdened by me on your long trip?"

"Not at all," Barnabas said. "I'll have a much more peaceful mind knowing you are not in this house."

"When can you book passage on a vessel?" she asked.

"There is one sailing within the week," Barnabas told her. "I was planning on taking it. The Ocean Sprite bound for Boston. Shall I go ahead with bookings?"

Paula made a sudden decision. "Yes."

Aunt Lucy looked worried. "You're sure you'll be all right so far away from London?"

Paula went to her and placed an arm around her. "It will be a fine change for me, and you can have the house waiting for me when I return. I wouldn't leave if I couldn't entrust it to you."

The old woman looked pleased. "You can depend on me, child. But I shall be lonely without you."

Barnabas was on his feet. "She need only stay in America a few months. By then I'm reasonably sure they'll have arrested Bentley and it will be safe for her to come back."

There followed a lively discussion of their plans and the clothes Paula should take along. At last Aunt Lucy grew weary and decided to go up to bed. As she stood leaning on her cane before going out of the room, she gave Barnabas a shrewd glance. "I hope I can trust you with my niece, Mr. Collins," she said sharply.

Barnabas smiled. "Depend on it."

"There have been tales told about you and some of your strange friends in London," the old woman reminded him.

"Nothing too blackening of my character, I trust."

The old woman looked grim. "I must say you have been a tower of strength since Sir Phillip's murder. Before that I was extremely dubious about you. And I warn you, if anything should happen to Paula you will have to answer to me!"

Paula went to her with a smile. "You're being needlessly dramatic, Aunt Lucy. Barnabas will take excellent care of me."

"He had better," was Aunt Lucy's final comment before she made her way out of the room.

When she'd gone, Paula turned to Barnabas with a look of apology. "She has failed greatly since my father's passing. You will notice that she now uses a cane and before she was so vigorous. Forgive her childish doubts about you."

Barnabas smiled. "I don't blame her for being concerned regarding your welfare."

Her brown eyes met his deep-set ones and she asked softly, "Why don't we travel to America as wife and husband? Marry me,

Barnabas. You know it is what I want."

He stared at her sadly. "It is also what I want; you should be aware of that. But at the moment it isn't possible. We must be content with merely being friends."

"But you will be cured," she pleaded. "You've not given up hope?"

"No," he said. "We can worry about that later."

"But you mustn't give up," she said. "You owe it to me and to yourself to find the antidote to that awful curse."

"That is always in my mind," he said soberly. "Now I must say goodnight. Bright and early tomorrow I'll set about making arrangements for the voyage. I'll write to Cousin James and inform him you'll be arriving with me."

Her eyes were bright with excitement. "You've told me so much about Collinsport and Collinwood. I'm looking forward to seeing them."

"We'll take a train from Boston to Maine," Barnabas told her. "The service is new and they make two trips a week."

"How long will the train journey take?"

"A full day and part of the evening," Barnabas said. "Or we may find it expedient to take the night boat instead. It calls directly at Collinsport and it might be the better way. I'll make inquiries in Boston."

She accompanied him to the door and they said goodnight. Barnabas gave her a parting kiss, and then went on his way. Sergeant Snell had removed the police officer on duty in the house several days before, but he'd promised to have an extra guard patrolling the square.

As she moved toward the curving stairway down which Jabez had hurled her father to his death, she saw Ebbets coming out of the shadowed hallway.

The butler bowed to her. "Your guest has left, Miss Sullivan?"

"Yes," she said. "You can lock up for the night."

"I will make the final check," he promised. He had been warned by the police to be extremely careful.

"Thank you, Ebbets." She started up the spiral stairway.

It was when she reached the landing that she had the first sensation of fear. It came on her without warning and apparently without any valid reason. She stood there in the wide hallway with its darkness broken only by the candle she held in her hand. The flickering glow of the tiny flame cast her shadow on the wall.

She stared ahead of her into the blackness and debated returning downstairs and asking Ebbets to make a search of the corridor and the rooms off it. She seemed to sense an intruder there... an intruder from the world of the supernatural.

It made her angry with herself. She had never been one to have childish terrors of the dark and the apparitions which might be lurking in the shadows. But now the skeleton fingers of fear touched her spine and sent a phantom chill down it. She hesitated for a moment and then forced herself to walk on with the candle held high.

Reaching her room, she found Emma there. The maid had been extremely upset since the night of the murder and as a result Paula no longer had her sleep in her room but let her go to the servants' quarters after she'd finished the bedtime chores.

Emma offered her a timorous smile of greeting. "I've taken care of everything, miss."

Paula noted the turned-down bed, the candle lighted on the dresser and the steaming pitcher of hot water on the commode. She turned to the maid and gave her the candle she'd been carrying. "This will light you down."

"Thank you, miss," Emma said, taking the candle. "Is there anything else?"

"No. Goodnight, Emma."

"Goodnight, miss." The maid quickly left and closed the door quietly after her.

Alone in her room, she again felt the threat of the menacing unknown and began to wonder whether there was someone outside watching the house again. Quickly she crossed to the window and pushed aside the drapes to stare down into the fog-shrouded square.

There was no one in sight, and yet her tension grew. Fearfully she turned and gazed about the shadowed room. She had the feeling she was not alone. Her eyes wandered to the door of the clothes closet and she saw that it was slowly opening!

The sight froze her body and voice. Completely paralyzed by her fear, she stood there with her eyes fixed on the moving door. And then from the dark depths of the closet a figure emerged. It was Lily, the female vampire with the painted face.

Lily's eyes were glowing strangely and she stood there with her shabby shawl around her shoulders, her fuzzy hair askew as usual. With a wise smile, she said, "Hello, luv!"

"What are you doing here?" Paula managed at last.

"I've been sent," Lily said mockingly.

"Who sent you?"

"Bentley! Who else?"

Paula frowned. "Why did he tell you to come here?"

Lily drew the shawl more tightly around her and ambled across the room, taking in all its details. "This is a swank place. Not the sort I'm used to! No wonder you didn't take to Cannon Lane."

Paula followed her to the dresser where Lily stood admiring

herself in the oval mirror. "Why did Bentley have you come to me?"

Lily turned her painted face to her and with a bitter smile said, "Would you look at that, luv? Not a trace of me in the mirror!"

Paula gazed into the mirror and saw she was right. Only Paula's reflection appeared in the glass. Startled, she asked, "Why?"

"Our lot can't see themselves in mirrors," Lily said with amused irony. "Maybe it's just as well. A face gets worn after a century."

She couldn't hide her amazement. "You're saying you're more than a hundred years old?"

Lily smiled smugly. "A woman never tells her age. I'm not about to make an exception."

"You can let me hear why Bentley sent you," she insisted.

"He wants you to know you can't escape him."

Paula lifted her chin independently. "We'll see about that!"

"I wouldn't try to cross him if I were you."

"But you're not me," Paula reminded her. With the sight of Lily, some of her fear had vanished but now she began to feel it return. After all, the woman standing there so calmly was a phantom! A ghost!

Or, at least, close to one. Barnabas was in the same sad state, but he had never seemed repulsive or frightening to Paula. Perhaps it was because he had such a kind and charming personality.

Lily winked at her and continued her rounds of the bedroom. "Bentley isn't so awful when you get to know him, luv!"

"Don't tell me that!" Paula exclaimed, realizing more and more clearly that Barnabas had been right. London was not safe for her.

Lily turned to stare at her with those weirdly glittering eyes again. And moving toward her, she said, "You don't want a feud with him, luv. Best to make up. Be wise and you'll live a lot longer. He has a fancy for that pretty face of yours. I'll be willing to wager he would marry you if you played your cards right!"

"Marry him! I'd sooner die! I think he's despicable!"

"You don't want me to tell him that, luv!"

Terror flared up in Paula. She backed away from the painted, smiling face of Lily. "Don't come near me!"

Lily chuckled. "I won't hurt you, luv. Bentley told me I mustn't. But I do want to just touch my lips to that soft throat of yours!"

And she lunged forward before Paula could escape and sank her teeth in her velvet throat!

CHAPTER 8

It was dawn! Paula stirred a little on the carpet where she'd fallen when Lily had let her go. The fog which had cloaked her mind since the attack of the vampire was now passing from her. She raised herself on an elbow and glanced around with glazed, frightened eyes. She was alone! Lily had vanished as easily as she had appeared.

Paula raised exploring fingers to her throat. It was stinging as it had before. But Lily had been cautious; she'd only taken a small quantity of blood from her and not drained her arteries to leave her a vampire. Another time it might be different!

She got up from the floor, walked shakily over to the bed, and stretched out with the eiderdown puff drawn over her. She was still there sleeping when an astonished Emma came to help her with her morning toilet a few hours later. Paula said merely that she'd been too exhausted to undress. She'd fallen asleep before she realized it. And she was careful to hide the tell-tale mark on her neck as much as she could.

But as Emma helped her with her hair, she said, "I'm going away for a while, Emma. I have made up my mind."

The maid was distressed. "Oh, no, miss!"

She nodded, studying her pale face in the mirror. "I must, Emma. London is no longer safe for me. I need to get away."

"When will you come back?"

"One day," she said quietly. "It's hard to say now."

"Everyone will be sad to hear the news, miss," Emma promised her. "What with the master being killed and all."

"Aunt Lucy will supervise the household," Paula said. "She will make a kind mistress to you all. And I am going with Barnabas to visit the new world of America."

The Ocean Sprite set sail for Boston on a dawn of driving rain. If the weather were a portent of what lay ahead, then the prospects were surely evil... but Paula did not believe this was true. She had boarded the vessel the previous night with Barnabas. His loutish servant, Willie Loomis, had come with him and supervised the installation of a certain coffin-like box in his cabin.

The night had been pleasant enough and she and Barnabas had walked the decks of the ship talking of their plans. It was then she told him for the first time of the midnight visit of Lily to her bedroom and the narrow escape she'd had. Barnabas listened with a frown.

"So Bentley sent her to bring his message," he said.

"Yes."

His handsome face showed anger. "If it weren't that I wanted to get you out of England quickly, I'd settle with Dr. Nicholas Bentley."

They were standing by the railing and she touched his arm. "Let us try to forget about him and all the madness he stands for. In America we will have left the resurrectionists behind."

"In name only," Barnabas warned her. "As long as bodies are restricted for medical dissection over there, the same wicked traffic in them will go on."

"Surely not in a small center like Collinsport."

"No," he agreed. "We should be relatively safe there."

She looked up at him with tender eyes. "We'll find a new beginning."

"I hope so."

They had talked a little longer, and then he kissed her goodnight and left her at her cabin door. Now that dawn had come, she stood by the railing alone, wearing a cloak and bonnet as protection against the rain. Barnabas had retired to the coffin in his cabin with the advent of day. It would be evening before they could be together again; meanwhile his servant would stand guard on the cabin. As she gazed at the receding coastline of England through the heavy rain, she knew a great feeling of relief. Perhaps now it would be happier for her and Barnabas.

Her hopes were still high when she reached the harbor of Collinsport on a quite different and smaller ship. The side-wheeler which Barnabas had chosen to be their transportation from Boston to the small Maine coastal village ended their long journey, except for the carriage ride to Collinwood.

They arrived at Collinwood after midnight. It was not until the next morning that she got her first clear impressions of the rambling, forty-room house and its surroundings. It was a large estate with a fine view of the ocean from its site on the high cliffs.

James and Maria Collins were on hand to greet her at breakfast. They were quiet middle-aged folk and childless. James had a short gray beard and pale blue eyes behind gold-rimmed spectacles, while Maria was a pleasant, fat dumpling of a woman.

"We want you to enjoy your stay here." Maria smiled at her across the breakfast table. "Barnabas did not tell us that you were so attractive."

James Collins nodded his agreement. "Since we have no children of our own, it is a delight to have young people in the house."

"Thank you," she said. "It is so lovely here."

Maria warned her, "You will find it a rough country, much different from England. But the people are friendly when you get to know them."

"Later you must visit our fish-packing plant," James Collins said. "We are near the wharf in the village and each year salt a great many shipments of fish for the West Indies trade."

"It sounds interesting," Paula said.

"The family established the business when they came here nearly a half-century ago," he said. "We hope to see it continue to grow with the years."

She said, "Barnabas chose to go to England rather than remain in the family business?"

Maria gave her husband a nervous glance. "I suppose you could say that."

James Collins coughed embarrassedly. "We do not pretend to understand Barnabas or his way of life," the middle-aged man said. "We tolerate him and ask no questions. But he is no longer close to the family."

"He seems very fond of what he calls the old house," Paula said, still attempting to discuss Barnabas in a pleasant fashion, but becoming aware that this might be difficult.

"The old house was built by his father years ago," James Collins said. "It was left for his use whenever he cares to visit here. Lately he has not come often."

She received the impression that he might have preferred it if Barnabas didn't visit them at all. Did they know his tragic secret? Were they afraid of him? Perhaps this explained their attitude.

Later, when James had left for the fish-packing plant, Maria showed her through the great mansion. And in the entrance foyer Paula discovered the fine portrait of Barnabas.

Staring at it with admiration, she said, "He is truly handsome."

The stout Maria regarded her with worried eyes. "May I ask a very personal question? Are you in love with him?"

She sighed. "I think so."

"Be careful!" Maria warned her. "Don't be carried away by your emotions. I doubt if Barnabas will ever want to marry and settle down. I wouldn't like to see your heart broken by him."

Paula smiled. "I'm aware of the risks of a romance with him."

"There are many risks," Maria said with a hint of mystery in her manner. Then she took Paula out to see the rose gardens.

It was a pleasant, sunny day and Paula elected to take a walk along the cliffs after her hostess had returned to the house. The path was close to the edge of the high cliffs; the tide coming in below roared and beat against the rocks, leaving an eddy of swirling foam and water each time. Maria had told her of a high point known as Widows' Hill about a half-mile from Collinwood. She decided to walk that far and then back.

She was anxious to talk to Barnabas but knew there was no chance of this until the evening. From what Maria and her husband had said, it seemed likely they knew that Barnabas suffered under a vampire curse though they did not care to talk about it. Here in the peaceful countryside she and Barnabas would have plenty of time to discuss his problem and try to find a solution for it.

At last she reached the jutting high point of the cliffs and was able to admire the wide vista, which included the village on the left, the bay before her, and another arm of land with a lighthouse to her right. Barnabas had described the area so that she recognized most of the landmarks.

Her eyes dropped to the rocky beach below and she was startled to see a couple down there. The young man had the girl in his arms obviously kissing her. Paula was embarrassed, feeling as if she was spying, even though it was purely accidental.

The young man glanced up and she was sure he saw her. She at once drew back from the edge of the cliff. Though it was quite a distance down to where the two were standing, she had seen them plainly and thought she would recognize them if she met them again. She wondered if they would know her.

Wondering who the two morning romantics might be, she started slowly walking back toward Collinwood. She'd not gone any distance when she heard footsteps hurrying behind her. And a moment later a breathless young man, fashionably dressed and with long brown sideburns and wavy hair, came up beside her. It needed only a glimpse of his good-looking face to know he was the fellow from the beach.

He said, "I've been racing to catch up with you."

Paula considered him primly. "May I ask why?"

His eyes held a roguish gleam. "I saw you spying on us from Widows' Hill."

"I was not spying!"

He shrugged. "Call it whatever you like. You were staring down at me while I was kissing that girl."

Paula blushed at his frankness. "Sir, whatever you do on the beach is no concern of mine."

The young man laughed. "I swear you must be a Collins. Some relation to James and Maria, though I can't imagine which branch of the family you represent."

"I'm a guest of Mr. and Mrs. Collins and I'll thank you not to detain me longer with your idle talk," she said coldly and started on.

"Wait a moment," the young man implored her. "I very much want you to like me. And I have something to explain."

She marched on, her eyes straight ahead. "I can't imagine anything you'd have to say that I'd want to hear!"

He hurried ahead of her and then blocked her way. With an expression of concern he said, "Please, listen to me for a moment."

"You are in my way."

"I want you to hear me out."

"I could scream for help," she said. "Someone at Collinwood is bound to hear me and come to my aid."

He looked forlorn as he glanced over his shoulder at the mansion towering a distance behind them and then at her. "I haven't a doubt they'd rescue you all right. And they'd like nothing better than to order me from the grounds."

She eyed him coldly. "Well then?"

"You wouldn't cause me all that trouble."

"Don't tempt me."

"Listen to me," he said. "I'm one of the Collins family. If you're a friend of James and Maria, there's no reason why you shouldn't also include me. I'm a cousin and my name is Quentin Collins."

She was suspicious. "How do I know that's true?"

"It is. They'll verify it if you ask them. And they'll also tell you what a reckless scamp I am. You see, I have a rather bad name in family circles. In spite of what a pleasant person I am, they think even less of me than they do of Barnabas."

Paula couldn't conceal her astonishment. "You know Barnabas?"

The man who called himself Quentin Collins laughed. "Of course I do. He is also my cousin. He's living in England just now."

"You're wrong," she said with triumph. "He is not in England. He has come to visit at Collinwood and is staying at the old house."

It was his turn to reveal astonishment. "Barnabas is back?"

"Yes."

He seemed amused by this news. "That ought to make things really lively," he said. "Both of us here at the same time."

"What do you mean?"

He was studying her closely. "I take it you are a friend of Barnabas."

"I am. He brought me here from England with him."

Quentin whistled. "What do you know? And yet you're abroad in the daytime! I would have expected you to sleep by day and appear by night. That's the way cousin Barnabas lives. But you must be aware of that, if you are close friends."

"I don't question his way of living or his reasons for it."

"You're a most interesting girl," the young man said with admiration.

"You can spare me your opinions," she said. And with a toss of her head, she inquired, "May I go on my way now?"

"In a moment," he said. "After I explain what you saw when you were spying on me on the beach."

Her cheeks crimsoned. "I wasn't spying!"

He ignored this. "The young woman you saw kissing me is a fisherman's daughter. She, for some reason, has taken a mad liking for me. I can't rid myself of the tiresome little thing. And when I take my daily walk along the beach she invariably runs out from her house, which is near the beach a short way back, and throws her arms around me. Naturally I'm defenseless."

"Naturally."

"The pretty little vixen is trying to compromise me," he fretted. "And you have an example of what her game is. See how she has made you feel about me."

"I have no feelings about you at all, Mr. Collins," she said in an even tone. "I only wish to continue on to the house."

"In due time," he said, still blocking her way. "I'm telling you all this because I don't want you to think wrong about me."

"My eyesight is excellent, Mr. Collins," she said. "And I saw it was you who had her in your arms."

He smiled apologetically. "In the end I guess maybe I was caught up in her emotion and carried away."

"I'm sure you must have been," she said. "Good morning, Mr. Coffins."

"Good morning, my dear," he said, stepping aside at last to let her pass. "We'll meet again and soon. I'm certain of it."

"Not if I have anything to say about it," Paula said and moved on quickly. The young man did not follow her. And when she looked back a little later he was gone.

Reaching the safety of the mansion, she went inside and found Maria busily crocheting. As the stout woman looked up, her hook still darting in and out of the thread, she asked her, "Do you know a Quentin Collins?"

Maria lowered her work, her fat face a study in confusion. "Quentin Collins?"

"Yes."

Maria swallowed uneasily. "Yes. I know him. He is distantly related to my husband. Why do you ask?"

"I just met him."

"Where?"

"Here. On the grounds. He was on the beach kissing some fisherman's daughter," she said with exasperation.

"It sounds like him," Maria said gloomily. "I had heard he'd left the village, but I suppose it was too much to hope for."

Paula stared at the older woman. "Why do you talk of him that way?"

Maria looked vexed. "He has caused the family a great deal of trouble. No one can manage him, and the villagers distrust him. It makes it very awkward for all of us."

"He seems pleasant enough."

"He has a fatal attraction for young women," the fat woman said mournfully. "Let me warn you against him."

"I have no interest in him at all," she said too casually. She knew he'd aroused her curiosity or she wouldn't have been asking all those questions about him.

"With Barnabas back, it makes it truly difficult," Maria said, picking up her crocheting again.

"Why should their being here at the same time mean anything?"

"They are the black sheep of our family," Maria said. "I'm sorry, but that is the truth."

Since Maria was obviously not going to explain herself, Paula could hardly wait for dusk, when she would be able to question Barnabas about it. To save time she left Collinwood after dinner and walked along the path by the stables to the shuttered red brick structure known as the old house.

When she mounted the steps, and knocked, she wondered if Barnabas would answer the door. He didn't. It was Willie Loomis who showed his head with ludicrous caution in the doorway.

"Where is Barnabas?" she asked.

"He's busy."

"I'm sure he must be awake now," she insisted. "I want to see him."

"Why don't you wait for him at Collinwood?" Willie suggested.

"Because I want to talk to him now."

Willie looked unhappy. He still blocked the doorway. "He ain't here."

"But he must be," she insisted. "Dusk settled only a few minutes ago. He can't have more than risen from his bed."

The youth glowered at her. "I told you he ain't here!"

"Then where is he?"

Willie hesitated. "You won't go to him anyway."

She was becoming exasperated. "I asked you to tell me where he is at this moment!"

The loutish youth stared at her. "He's in the cemetery."

"In the cemetery?"

"The old one. Down there." He pointed toward a sloping field.

"You're not playing a prank on me, are you?" she asked nervously.

"No, miss. That's where he is."

"Very well," she said, feeling some misgivings as he closed the door on her again. She stood there for a moment trying to make up her mind what to do.

Then her need to talk to Barnabas overcame her apprehensions and she began slowly walking down the sloping field in the twilight. It would soon be dark and she worried about being out there alone. The place was still strange to her, and a graveyard was not the most pleasant of destinations in the blue half-light.

As she reached the bottom of the field she saw the iron fence surrounding the cemetery and found the open gate leading inside. A chill of fear ran through her as she entered the grim resting place of the Collins dead.

Where could Barnabas be? And how had he gotten here so soon after rising from his coffin at the old house? There could barely have been time for him to leave and get this far. She moved on between the gravestones which flanked her like ghosts on either side.

Darkness was approaching fast. The wind rustled through the tall evergreens at the rear of the cemetery. She came to a halt and shuddered. It had been a mistake for her to come to such an isolated spot with night approaching. She would have been wiser to have waited at the old house. Willie would have surely let her in.

She wanted to turn and rush out of the cemetery, but she was too stricken with unreasoning fear to move. She stood there not knowing what to do next. Then she heard a quick movement behind her in the dark. She wheeled around only to see the mocking gray faces of the gravestones. And yet she knew she had heard something!

Glancing around, she tried to convince herself it was only her nerves, but she was taut and sick with terror. And now the sound came again—a furtive, quick movement.

She screamed and ran deeper into the graveyard. In her flight she stumbled and fell beneath a gnarled old tree, not yet in leaf, whose grotesque twisted arms stood out against the darkening sky like the arms of tormented spirits.

As she started to get up from the damp grass, she saw in the distance, between the headstones, two blazing eyes. Two eyes, of yellow flame! She screamed again, and getting up, began a frantic, senseless flight toward the area of the graveyard where several large tombs stood.

Sobbing hysterically, she fell exhausted against the iron door of one of the tombs. And she saw those weird, blazing eyes again—coming nearer her! And as they drew close, she made out the huge wolf-like body behind them. The snarling creature came within a dozen feet of her and crouched as if ready to spring.

Frantic, she screamed and rattled the iron tomb doors. To her surprise one of them fell open and automatically she dodged back into the fetid blackness and closed the iron door behind her, against the menacing wild thing outside. She had never seen anything like it and could only imagine it was native to this country so new to her.

She leaned against the door, gasping for breath. Her terror increased as she heard the animal snuffling and moving about outside. She dare not leave this place of the dead. She was trapped in the tomb!

Even the sound of her own breathing, difficult and loud, was unnerving in the confined area of the tomb. It seemed strangely quiet outside, but she didn't dare let herself hope the phantom thing with the burning eyes had gone.

She would have to wait longer. But could she? Now the oppressive atmosphere of the dark tomb began to take its toll from her. With the danger outside at least temporarily at bay, she was becoming aware of the horror of the surroundings to which she had so quickly abandoned herself.

Her eyes were gradually becoming adjusted to the blackness; now she could make out the shelves on either side of the tomb. Three to a side, with adequate space between them for the placement of caskets. And all of the shelves were filled; the caskets they held must be cobwebbed and dusty. Each of those six long boxes must contain skeletons with mocking skull faces. The grin of death!

She tried to get her mind off these morbid thoughts by thinking about what was outside. She was safe behind the protection of the rusty tomb door. Out there she'd be defenseless before the snarling beast with its yellow fangs and blazing eyes.

Better to remain with the dead. She drew a deep sigh. And almost at once she thought she heard a similar sigh in return. It appeared to come back to her from the rear of the tomb, where the six caskets loomed in the darkness. But it was impossible! It couldn't be! Just another trick of her overwrought nerves.

Then the creaking sound came. Very slowly. A thin creaking, like the opening of hinges long without oil. Rusty hinges, such as might be on the lid of a coffin! She sobbed at the thought. No! She mustn't allow herself to go on that way. But the sound continued and then there was a soft moan.

She backed against the iron door, her eyes fixed on a coffin on the lower shelf to the left of her. And she saw that its lid had been swung open. Before her terrified eyes there was a shadow of motion inside the ancient casket. Fear such as she had never known before surged through her. Hypnotized with horror, she continued gazing at the tomb in the murky shadows and very slowly a hand lifted and began to grope along the side of the casket!

She pictured a thin, mummified corpse raising itself from the grimy interior of the casket and coming groping toward her in blind and fetid loathesomeness. It was too much! Ignoring the possible danger outside, she wrenched open the rusty iron door and scrambled up the uneven moss-ridden steps to the fresh night air.

Again she ran frantically in what she thought was the proper direction to find the cemetery gates. The wolflike creature with the blazing eyes appeared to have vanished. But in its place to torment her was the dread vision of the casket opening and the withered hand rising from it.

Frantically she ran on, only to find herself at a dead end. The fence at this point was high with a spiked top. She couldn't get over it. There was nothing for her to do but turn and retrace her steps. Heart pounding madly, she made her way back amid the forest of gravestones.

It was then she heard the footsteps running toward her. She didn't wait to see who it was, she had a vision of the horror that had emerged from the coffin. The phantom was now coming after her. She was lost, thoroughly lost in this domain of the dead!

Sobbing, she hurried on. The thing behind her drew closer. Then she saw the open gate which offered her freedom from the terror. She felt a burst of hope. But in that same instant she stumbled and fell, sprawling forward with a great sob. And the hand of the phantom was on her!

CHAPTER 9

"Paula!" It was Barnabas.

She turned and looked up into his concerned face. "You!" she gasped.

"Yes," he said, taking her by the arms and helping her to her feet. "You gave me a wild chase. I thought I'd never catch up with you."

Disheveled and breathless, still not over her terror, she stood there staring at him. "It was you behind me all the time?"

He nodded. "I called out to you but you didn't seem to hear."

"I was too frightened."

"You shouldn't have come here alone."

"I came to find you," she said, as they stood facing each other in the dark cemetery. "Then a weird animal came after me and I hid in a tomb. While I was in it a coffin opened and a terrifying phantom figure emerged from it."

Barnabas offered her a bitter smile. "That terrifying phantom was me. I sometimes go to my father's tomb. It is filled with members of our family. Once long ago I was chained by my father in that very coffin you saw me leave. He hoped in that way I would never be free to wander the earth as a vampire."

"You!" She found it hard to believe.

"I didn't mean to frighten you," he apologized. "When I first awaken I am not always aware of my surroundings or those near me.

If you'd waited a minute before running away, I would have identified myself."

"Willie said you were in the cemetery," she recalled, "but he didn't explain that you were spending the night here in a coffin."

"Would you expect him to do that?"

"No. I suppose not."

"I'm sorry," Barnabas said. "Are you feeling better?"

"Yes."

He was studying her with interest. "What about this weird animal you mentioned?"

"I don't know," she said, fear crossing her face at the remembrance of it. "I've never seen such a creature before. It was like a wolf, yellowish-gray in color, with blazing amber eyes."

"There are no wolves in this area," Barnabas said. "But what you saw could well have been a threat of a different sort. I'd expect it if I were certain my cousin, Quentin Collins, was in the area."

Her eyes widened. "But he is!"

"He is?"

"Yes."

"How do you know?"

"I met him earlier today," she said. And then she gave him a full account of the meeting.

Barnabas listened intently. "It was Quentin, without a doubt." His eyes met hers. "You have heard of his suffering from the werewolf curse?"

"Only vague hints of something wrong," she said.

"Well, he does," Barnabas went on. "Without question it was he who first scared you here tonight. He often does this sort of thing. It pleases his sense of humor."

Her brow furrowed. "You're suggesting the beast I saw was Quentin. And that he deliberately frightened me!"

"It's very likely the truth," Barnabas admitted.

"How dare he!" she stormed.

He smiled faintly. "You'll rarely find him considerate."

"This was a dreadful thing to do," she went on in the same note.

"You found him interesting when you met him earlier, I'll wager."

Paula was embarrassed. "Then I was very wrong about him."

"Not really," Barnabas told her. "Quentin can be charming when he likes. The trouble is he is far from stable. Every so often he does something that brings disgrace on both himself and the family."

"So that is why Maria Collins was so upset to hear that he had come back."

"Yes. They won't allow him here on the estate. He stays somewhere in the village. We've met in the Blue Whale Tavern occasionally when we've both been here at the same time."

"As you are now."

"Exactly. The truth is that James and Maria are wary of both Quentin and myself. They'd be happier if we didn't ever appear here."

"I gathered that," she admitted.

Barnabas smiled ruefully. "Birds of a feather, so they think. And yet both Quentin and I have done much for the Collins name in our own ways. We simply don't get credit for our good deeds, despite the full marks for our bad ones."

She gave a tiny shudder. "I'm beginning to think life will be as full of hazards here as it was back in London."

"Not quite," Barnabas said. "There is no Nicholas Bentley on the scene." He put an arm around her. "Come, I'll walk you back to Collinwood."

They walked up the hill to the old house and then on by the stables to the rambling Collinwood. Lights showed from its windows to welcome them.

Barnabas entered the mansion with her and they paused to study the painting of him in the foyer. She said, "I think it's excellent."

His deep-set eyes were sad as he gazed up at it. "So many years ago," he said.

James Collins came out to greet them. "I see you are with Barnabas," he said to her. "I was worried when I discovered you'd gone out alone."

"I'm sorry I caused you concern."

James looked grim. "Collinwood is not a good place to roam by yourself after dark." He glanced at Barnabas. "I'm sure you'll agree, though your own habits tend that way."

"It is different with me," Barnabas said soberly. And he told her, "You'd be wise to follow the suggestion James has made."

She gave him a meaningful look. "I realize that now," she said.

"Come into the drawing room," James invited them. "Maria is there."

The stout Maria was sitting working at some embroidery. When she saw Barnabas, she asked him, "Did you know Quentin is back?"

Barnabas smiled. "I just heard it from Paula. I was surprised."

"We all are. I think James should speak to him politely and ask him to leave," Maria said.

James Collins had taken a stand beside his wife's chair and now he stroked his short gray beard. "I don't like to interfere. In fact, I have no right to. And if Quentin should take offense at my saying such a thing to him he might be all the more ready to provoke trouble."

"That is a possibility," Barnabas agreed.

Maria looked at him anxiously. "What do you think we should

do?"

Barnabas smiled in his grim fashion. "I'm afraid there's no pat answer. We can only hope that Quentin will be quickly bored by the quiet village life and continue on his way."

"Providing some pretty girl doesn't catch his attention," Maria pointed out. "You'll remember what has happened before."

"Yes," Barnabas said. "I do remember."

Later, when Paula was saying goodnight to Barnabas at the front door, she asked him, "What did Maria mean by saying you should remember what happened with Quentin before?"

He looked grimly amused. "On several occasions Quentin has been smitten by some local beauty and stayed on here an unendurable time until the romance was broken by one or the other of them. We can hope it won't happen this visit."

Then Barnabas kissed her goodnight and promised to see her the following evening. But he warned her to wait at Collinwood for him and not wander out into the darkness on her own. She went up to bed thoroughly exhausted from her experiences.

It was not surprising that she fell into a terrifying nightmare in which the graveyard, Dr. Bentley and the snarling werewolf became all madly confused. When she woke in the morning the details of the nightmare were still with her, depressing her.

Since there had been no prohibition against her going out walking in the daytime, she decided she'd like to explore the beach for herself. In the early afternoon she took the path down the steep cliffs to the rocky beach and then she strolled along toward the base of Widows Hill.

She'd only gone a little distance when she rounded a huge boulder and discovered Quentin seated on the sand enjoying the sunshine. He got to his feet at once and smiled at her.

"I've been waiting for you to come," he said.

She stared at him in surprise. "How could you guess I'd be taking a walk along the beach?"

The good-looking young man smiled at her. "I invoked a magic spell to make you come this way."

She blushed. "Nonsense!"

He raised a protesting hand. "On the contrary, it is true."

Her eyes blazed at him. "I hear you are capable of some strange doings," she said. "But I'd hoped to be spared from them."

Quentin looked hurt. "And I so much want you to like me."

"I think you are idle and insolent," she informed him. "You waste your time and play cruel childish pranks on people."

He laughed. "Now that sounds familiar. You've been listening to Maria. That fat old prophet of doom despises me. And I doubt if her husband or Barnabas have anything to say in my favor."

"Barnabas was very fair about you," she said. "He probably is your best friend here."

Quentin arched an eyebrow. "Really? Are you sure that isn't pretense on his part? We are going to be rivals for your love, did you know that?"

Paula's cheeks flamed. "No insolence, please!"

"I mean it," Quentin said. "I have decided I am in love with you."

"From all I hear, and what I've seen, you fall in love very easily," she snapped at him.

"But this time is different," he insisted. "I shall woo you and win you from Cousin Barnabas. What do you say to that?"

"I will say that I think you are mad," Paula told him angrily.

And then he took her completely by surprise, folding his arms around her and drawing her to him for an ardent kiss, while she pounded him with her fists to release her. When he did let her go, he was laughing uncontrollably.

"Scoundrel!" she cried, stumbling back on the sand.

"Come now," he said. "Must you make so much fuss about a kiss!"

"I'm not one of your fisherman's girls!" she said, near sobbing. "You won't find me coming running for your kisses!"

Quentin looked ashamed. "I'm sorry," he said. "I shouldn't have done that. I followed an impulse."

"Just as you did in the cemetery last night!"

He looked taken back. "What about the cemetery?"

"Don't pretend!" she said angrily. "I know and so do you. I'll thank you to let me alone in the future, Quentin Collins!" And she turned and walked back towards the path as fast as she could.

"Paula! I'm sorry!" he called after her, but she pretended not to hear him.

In a few minutes she had reached the path and was making her way up to the cliffs again. Later she saw him walking dejectedly along the beach alone. From her vantage point on the edge of the cliffs she watched him without his knowing, and in spite of her annoyance, a smile crossed her face. For all his faults there was something likeable about him. Barnabas had been correct in that.

The days became weeks and the weeks months. Soon it was August and Paula was so much at home in the old mansion of Collinwood that she felt herself almost one of the family. Only an occasional letter from Aunt Lucy in London reminded her of the dark days she'd left behind. With Aunt Lucy's letters came remembrance of the grave robbers and the mad Dr. Bentley—all the evil happenings she needed to erase from her mind.

Barnabas was helpful, always the considerate friend. And

though he had done nothing about finding a cure for his condition, she was still hopeful that he would. Strangely, she had also built a kind of friendship with the dashing Quentin. Barnabas had encouraged it, though he teased her and claimed Quentin was remaining in Collinsport only because of his love for her.

It was an easy, pleasant life on the estate though occasionally shadowed by dark overtones which she did not fully understand. She would enter a room to find James and Maria Collins talking seriously between themselves, yet the moment they saw her the discussion would end. She had a feeling they were keeping certain facts from her.

Yet there was nothing to disturb this quiet new pattern of life she was enjoying until an unexpected caller arrived at Collinwood one rainy evening in early September. Paula was alone in the library reading. Barnabas had told her he would not call, as he was making a visit to Bangor, and she had no idea where the dashing Quentin might be. No doubt at the bar of the Blue Whale entertaining his many friends.

Maria and her husband were in the drawing room by the fireplace when the knocking came on the front door. Paula, in the room opposite, put down her book and hurried to the door to answer it. And when she opened it she couldn't believe her eyes. It was John Williams!

"John!" she exclaimed with delight.

"Paula! I have made a long journey to find you," the young doctor said. He was wearing a wide-brimmed hat and a cloak to protect him from the rain.

"Do come in," she said.

He stepped inside and took off his soaked hat. She saw that his face was still gaunt and his eyes as sad and burning as they had been since Jane had been abducted and cruelly murdered. He'd never gotten over that, obviously.

"Paula!" he said again. Taking her in his arms, he kissed her gently on the lips.

Slightly embarrassed, she said, "Do come in and meet James and Maria Collins, who have been so kind to me.

She made the introductions; the middle-aged couple seemed delighted at this extra visitor from London. They began to ask John a lot of questions, which he answered with good humor though he seemed tired and strangely preoccupied. Every so often he would turn to glance quickly at her.

James Collins took out his massive gold watch and looked at it. "Nine o'clock," he said. "Time for Maria and me to retire. But you mustn't mind us, Dr. Williams. You and Paula remain here and have a long talk."

John was also on his feet. He bowed. "Thank you."

"And you'll be our guest," James Collins said. "I won't take any arguments. Whether you stay for a week or a month, it's all the same. We are honored to have a London doctor in the house."

The young doctor looked embarrassed. "I don't really know what to say in the face of such kindness."

Maria smiled warmly. "Just do us the honor of remaining," she said. "That is all we ask."

James patted him on the shoulder. "Remember that, young man." And they went out of the room and up the stairs to bed.

When John Williams was alone with her in the candlelit drawing room, he approached her with a look of genuine distress on his hollow-cheeked face.

"Poor dear Paula," he said. "You have no idea why I have come this long way."

"No," she confessed.

"I need not involve a lot of words to explain," the young doctor said. "It wasn't until you left London that I realized how much you mean to me. With Jane lost to me, I have only been able to think of you. And I hope you will forgive my saying that I'd like you to consider marrying me."

"John!" she said, touched by his words and yet knowing she didn't love him. She would have to find a way to let him down gently without hurting him too deeply.

"But that is not my main concern at the moment," John went on in a troubled tone. "I have come to bring you bad news from London."

"What sort of bad news?" she asked. "Isn't Aunt Lucy all right? I had her last letter only the other day!"

His eyes showed his unhappiness. "No, she's fine. What I have come to warn you is that Dr. Nicholas Bentley and his servant Jabez are somewhere here in America."

She felt her throat constrict. "Here!"

"Yes. The London police traced them to New York City, and there they lost them. Of course, the fact is they hardly have the evidence to make any charges against them over here. So the two have reached comparative safety." He paused, then added, "And as a matter of course your safety is threatened."

Paula slumped down in a nearby chair. "That is bad news."

"I felt you should be warned," the young doctor said. "And I wanted to do it personally."

She looked up at him wanly. "You were always my best friend, John."

His gaunt face took on a warmer look. "I hope to be more than that to you one of these days, Paula."

To change the subject, she asked, "Do you really fear that Dr.

Bentley will come here after me?"

He nodded gravely. "It is very possible."

"All that awful business over again," she fretted. "What will I do? I don't feel equal to fighting him."

"I have come to be of what help I can."

"I appreciate that, John," she said.

"But others must be alerted," he went on. "Is Barnabas Collins still here?"

"Yes. I'll let him know tomorrow night."

"You see him regularly then?"

"I do," she said. "He lives in the old house only a little walk from here."

"I see," the young doctor said, his face clouded. "How has it been with him?"

"What do you mean?"

In the glow of a candelabra on the table, John's face seemed more haggard than ordinary. "I heard some rather strange stories about him in London."

"Gossip," she said shortly. "Barnabas is a fine person." She didn't know whether John had stumbled on Barnabas' secret or not, but she was not going to expose him.

"There was a woman," John said, "no better than she should be, and a close friend of his. I understand her name was Lily."

"I know about her," Paula said. "I've met her."

"Oh?" He raised his eyebrows.

"You need have no worries about Barnabas," Paula assured him. "He would be the last to let me down."

"Excellent," the young doctor said, without much enthusiasm.

She supposed that he was jealous of Barnabas and her feelings for him. This was understandable; she preferred to overlook it. She said, "If Bentley turns up I don't know what we'll do."

"Time enough to think about that if and when he does come," John said. "You can handle him in any case. You know that he is fond of you. Didn't he ask you to marry him?"

"He did," she said bitterly. "I was invited to become the bride of the patron of the grave robbers and the indirect murderer of my father. What a flattering offer!"

He sighed. "I know how it is. I feel the same bitterness about losing Jane."

"Of course you must," she agreed sympathetically.

He looked around the elegantly furnished room. "This is an imposing place. The Collins family must be tremendously wealthy."

"I think so," she said. "They have been so good to me.

"I hardly like to take advantage of their offer to remain here as their guest."

"You mustn't travel back to the village on this rainy night," she said. "And I'm sure they do want you to be their guest as long as you like. Have you any idea as to how much time you'll be spending in America?"

"Not yet," he said. "I can't neglect my practice too long. Winslow Hospital is short of surgeons, with the loss of your father and Bentley."

"I can imagine," she said. "And has the horrid traffic in dead bodies been halted in any way?"

"It is being done more quietly," he said. "But I fear it still goes on and will until the laws pertaining to dissection are changed."

She smiled sadly. "You and my father were martyred in attempting to bring about a change."

"It will come," John said. "It is bound to. But as a result Jane and your father are dead. And Bentley is a renegade. He's too good a doctor to lose, in spite of his crimes."

His words astonished her. "You sound as if you approved of him. Do you think he deserves leniency?"

"Do I? Oh, no," he said quickly. "That wasn't my intent at all."

And she knew this must be true; he had as much reason to hate Bentley as she did. "I know that," she said quietly.

She showed him up to his room and then went on to her own. It wasn't surprising that her dreams were filled with the evil face of Nicholas Bentley. He pursued her relentlessly in her nightmares and she awoke in the morning feeling tired and ill.

The day was fine, with warm sunshine after the heavy rain. She and John went walking together in the rose gardens of Collinwood, and she pointed out various interesting facts about the place. He listened politely but with no great interest in anything. Obviously he still hadn't recovered from Jane's murder.

After a while he excused himself and went into the house, saying he wanted to find some books he'd brought that he wanted to show her. But she had the feeling it was rather that he had wearied of her company and wanted to be alone for a little. He had become very aloof.

She was standing in the garden thinking about this when she heard a footstep behind her and turned to see a smiling Quentin standing there. She said, "How long have you been there?"

"Long enough."

"What does that mean?"

His smile was mocking. "To discover you have a new admirer."

She blushed. "Quentin, why must you always be so difficult? He is an old family friend of mine from London."

"He's obviously in love with you."

"Don't always try to read minds," she said. "You're really not that good at it."

Quentin looked hurt. "I suppose Barnabas is much wiser."

Paula laughed ruefully. "You're jealous of everyone I know. Even Barnabas."

"You don't fool me," Quentin said. "Barnabas is important to you."

"So would you be, if you weren't so brash."

"I'll try to do better," he said, his good humor returning. And glancing toward the house, he added, "That fellow is a queer one. Something about him that bothers me."

"He had a kind of breakdown after his wife was murdered by grave robbers in London."

"I heard the story from Barnabas," Quentin recalled. "So he is Dr. John Williams and Jane was his wife."

"Yes."

Quentin looked interested. "What has brought him here?"

"He came to give me a warning."

"About what?"

"That enemies of mine have come to America. It may be that they'll come here. I could be in danger of my life if they do."

Quentin arched an eyebrow. "Anyone who threatens you will have to deal with me first."

"And Barnabas," she said. "He saved my life in London. I shall never forget it. I'm fortunate to have him here as well."

Quentin looked scornful. "Barnabas sleeps all the day. He isn't much help then."

"Fortunately, most of the evil takes place at night." She summoned a wan smile. "And I can count on you during the day."

"You can count on me at all times," Quentin told her. "But I'm still worried about the doctor. There's something strange about him. I doubt if his mind is right yet."

"I don't think it is," she agreed. "It was a terrible experience for him and one bound to leave scars."

Quentin frowned. "What was the name of that other doctor? The villain who headed all the evil?"

"Nicholas Bentley," she said. "And he has a huge brown-skinned manservant named Jabez. He's very strange."

Quentin was staring at her. "When I came down the beach today, I passed the old castle that has been vacant for years. There's somebody living in it now. I saw a big brown man with a shaven head and odd blank eyes standing on one of the balconies."

CHAPTER 10

The skies over Collinwood darkened early that evening, and by seven a thunderstorm began. Great forked tongues of lightning cut through the black clouds to briefly illumine the bay. Thunder rolled ominously close and there were intermittent periods of rain. This was unfortunate for Paula, who had arranged to meet Quentin by the stables and go with him to consult Barnabas at the old house.

A few minutes after the storm began she slipped down the stairway and across the entrance hall. John Williams was in the drawing room with James and Maria Collins, so she was able to leave unnoticed. Once on the steps, she bent her head against the storm and crossed the lawn, heading for the path by the stables. Collinwood seemed at the center of the storm, and she began to wonder if she should turn back. Then she saw a figure dart out of the shadows and run toward her. As it came close she recognized Quentin. The flowing cape he was wearing was soaked with rain and his wavy hair was streaked against his forehead.

Seizing her arm, he shouted melodramatically, "All the elements have turned their fury against us tonight."

She nodded. "It's a savage storm."

Bending close, he said, "I hope Barnabas doesn't decide to wander in the storm. I've known him to do it."

"I can't bear to think of missing him," she worried, "It's too urgent that we talk to him."

"Have any trouble getting out of Collinwood?"

"No. They were talking and didn't see me."

"If James weren't such an unbending character I would have called for you. But seeing me would only throw him in a rage."

"It didn't matter," she told him, but her reply was lost in a loud clap of thunder.

The rain was still coming down hard as they reached the steps of the old house and knocked on the door. There was a short wait before Willie Loomis opened the door and peered out.

Quentin told him, "We're here to see Barnabas."

"Are you expected?"

"He'll want to see us," Paula told the youth. "You know I'm his friend."

"I'll see," Willie said and closed the door, keeping them waiting in the rain and storm.

Quentin smiled down at her grimly as the lightning cut a blue streak through the sky once more and held his wet cape over her. "It won't do much good but it's a gesture anyway."

As he spoke the door opened again and it was Barnabas. He showed concern at their being on the steps in the storm. Standing back he said, "Come in at once! That stupid Willie should have admitted you in the first place."

Paula said, "We had to come here. We needed to see you and couldn't depend on your coming to Collinwood on such a night. And in any case, Quentin couldn't have met with us there."

Barnabas gave Quentin a knowing look. "So you are mixed up in this?"

"I'm afraid so," he said, taking off his cape.

"Come down to the living room," Barnabas said. "I have a fire in the grate and with the shutters closed we'll not notice the storm so much there."

They followed him down the murky corridor and into the candlelit living room. In this room the thunder could scarcely be heard.

Barnabas showed them to chairs and then stood by the fireplace with an interested look on his handsome face. "I find it unusual to have you come here together for a visit."

"The circumstances warrant the unusual," Quentin assured him.

Barnabas looked at her. "Isn't it time you told me the details?"

There was despair in her tone as she said, "Nicholas Bentley is here and Jabez along with him."

Barnabas lifted his heavy black eyebrows. "You can't mean it!"

Quentin nodded grimly. "It's true enough. I saw Jabez on the balcony of the old castle and told Paula about it. She identified him at once. So I then went to the village and talked to old Snodgrass, the lawyer who has charge of the castle for its Boston owners."

"And?" Barnabas demanded.

"Bentley bought the castle a few days ago. He's already moved in. Snodgrass is under the impression he is going to offer a special sort of health treatment, but we know better. He's setting up some kind of black magic center."

Paula said, "And he'll be back to his horrible experiments to make the dead into his slaves."

"How could all this take place without our hearing about it?"

"There's something else you don't know," Paula told him. "John Williams came yesterday and he's staying at Collinwood."

"What brought him here?" Barnabas asked in surprise.

"To warn me about Bentley."

"Did he know he was at the castle?"

"No," she said. Her face was shadowed with concern. "John is still in a very strange mood. Sometimes I can't reach him at all. When I told him this afternoon that Bentley had arrived and was living in the old castle almost next to this estate, he didn't seem to take it in."

"What did he say?"

"When I repeated the information several times he appeared to accept it," she went on in a worried voice. "But he suggested that we wait and see what Dr. Bentley does. He claims Bentley is in love with me and will not harm me."

"Ridiculous!" Barnabas declared angrily. "Especially considering what happened to Jane."

"I agree," Quentin said.

"I told him I was going to consult you and plan some sort of campaign against the doctor to try and get him to leave here," she said. "And he told me that would be a mistake. It would only anger Bentley and make him a worse threat."

"I fail to see it," Barnabas said.

Quentin's expression was thoughtful. "It is my impression that Dr. John Williams has lost his mind. His intentions in warning Paula against Bentley were good, but he is not able to work against Bentley and his evil. Bentley broke him when he murdered his wife. He has no nerves left."

Paula sighed. "I'm inclined to agree with you."

Barnabas pursed his lips as he stood lost in thought. Then he said, "It seems to me we'll have to forget all about John Williams in this. What is done will have to be done by the three of us."

"No question of it," Quentin said.

"It might be well to learn what Bentley is up to," Barnabas continued. "And Paula will have to be especially cautious from now on."

"I intend to be," she assured them.

Barnabas gave her a warning look. "And even that may not be enough. As long as Bentley lives you are threatened."

Quentin rose from his chair. "May I offer a suggestion?"

"Go on," Barnabas said.

Quentin smiled coldly. "I think we should destroy Bentley and that mad servant."

Paula gasped. "That's murder!"

"In this case?" Quentin demanded angrily. "It is more the sentence of the court, which the court is unable to carry out."

Barnabas said quietly, "Talking of killing Bentley and Jabez is one thing. Managing it is quite another."

"You feel it will be difficult?" Quentin said.

Barnabas shrugged. "You know the castle. It is built like a fortress of the Middle Ages. If Bentley arms himself and his followers he can remain in there as long as he likes."

Paula said, "The thing to do would be attack when he doesn't expect it."

"That might be next to impossible," Barnabas said.

"At least we can try," Quentin urged.

"Give me tonight to think about it and make plans," Barnabas said. "If we three stay together we should be able to accomplish something."

Paula was also standing now. "And you don't want me to say anything to John?"

"No," Barnabas said. "Better to keep young Dr. Williams in the dark. He's in no fit shape to stand up to the strain of a murder plot."

Quentin smiled bleakly. "I note that you are thinking of acting on my suggestion. Very good."

"That remains to be seen."

"I suppose we should leave now," Paula said worriedly. "I'd like to get back in without being missed."

Barnabas said, "They keep a close watch on you."

"Maybe that's for the best, the way things are," she suggested.

"Without a doubt," Quentin agreed in his enthusiastic way. Winking at her, he told Barnabas, "By the way, Dr. Williams is not so demented that he has not been able to tell Paula he still loves her. He asked her to return to England and marry him."

"Is that so, Paula?" Barnabas asked her.

She hesitated and then admitted, "Yes."

Barnabas gave her one of his sad smiles. "Perhaps you could do worse. I think I suggested it once before."

"And I turned the idea down," she said firmly.

"Well, at least we know where the doctor stands," Barnabas

said. "Make use of him as a protector. You can't have too many on your side. It is hard to say who Bentley has working for him."

Quentin seemed impatient of all the talk. "When do we meet again and get something done?"

"Here. Tomorrow night," Barnabas said. "We'll discuss various plans and go ahead with the one that pleases us all the most."

Quentin said, "I'll be here."

"And so shall I," Paula promised.

"At dusk," Barnabas said with a weary smile. "And don't allow Willie to turn you away. I'll inform him you're coming."

Quentin gave them both a mocking glance. "I don't think you two need me any longer. Will it distress you if I go on my way? I'd like to visit the village and pick up what information I can."

Barnabas nodded. "Go ahead. I'll escort Paula back to Collinwood."

"I was certain you'd take on the chore," Quentin teased him. And with a parting smile he left the room, his black cape on his shoulders.

When they were alone in the living room, she said, "Quentin can be wonderful and yet he's so unpredictable."

Barnabas smiled. "You seem to have won his heart. He's behaving much better than ever before. In fact, I'm shocked, he's becoming such a model character."

She sighed. "I'm terrified knowing that Bentley is so near. And he has surely followed us."

"No question of it." Barnabas frowned. "These last few nights I've had a strange feeling that danger was near. A sort of instinctive warning of the supernatural I sometimes get. This Bentley is dabbling in voodoo and I'm certain we'll be partly dealing with evil spirits."

"Jabez is surely a zombie," she said with a shudder.

"And there may be more like him," Barnabas said seriously. "We know that Bentley was trying to create zombies through the serum he'd evolved. Undoubtedly that is what has brought him here. To continue his experiments, and to eliminate you either by marrying you and binding you to him, or by destroying you."

"Either alternative would be fatal."

"I agree," Barnabas sighed. "I must give it all some thought. Now I will take you home."

All that was left of the storm was a drizzle of rain. Barnabas kissed her goodnight at the door and waited until she was safely inside. Everyone seemed to have gone to bed. She quietly made her way up the stairs to her own floor.

She was walking down the dark corridor to her room when she heard the floorboard creak behind her. She turned quickly, ready to scream, when she saw that it was John Williams in dressing gown with a lighted candle in his hand.

Holding the candle to cast its flickering glow on her face, he whispered, "Where were you?"

"I had to talk with Barnabas," she told him, believing he'd guess the truth no matter what she said.

His dark-circled eyes bore into her. "You went to see him about Bentley?"

She hedged. "I mentioned it."

"And about my being here?"

"Of course," she said. "You didn't want your arrival kept a secret, did you? We talked quite a lot about you."

John looked annoyed. "I'd rather you didn't discuss me when you're with him. You know we're rivals for your hand."

"Please don't begin that again," she pleaded.

"It's true," the young doctor said. "I worried when I found you had gone somewhere. Anything could happen to you on a night like this!"

"I went straight to the old house," she said. "It isn't far."

"I don't think you should go there again," John Williams told her, his haggard face seeming more emaciated in the light of the flickering candle.

"I must make my own decisions about that," she warned him. She was sorry for him and his confused state, but she didn't intend to let him dominate her with his weakness.

"James and Maria don't approve of your friendships with Barnabas or Quentin," he said sullenly. "And I don't either."

"I'm weary," she said. "Can't we talk about this tomorrow?"

His hollow eyes fixed on her suspiciously. "You're not telling me everything. I know that."

"Goodnight, John!" she said, dismissing him and his attempt to start another argument. Then she went into her own room.

It had not been an easy day or evening. Word that Bentley was living at the old castle had come as a shattering shock. Now she must try to find some way to protect herself from the evil madman. She couldn't think of him as anything else but mad. No matter how clever a surgeon he'd once been, he was now only interested in his macabre attempts to create zombies and his witchcraft gatherings.

There was a lighted candle on her dresser and she went over to look at herself in the mirror as she removed her cloak. She saw that she had a host of tired lines on her usually smooth face. Only sound sleep and freedom from fear would eliminate them.

As she stared into the mirror another figure appeared in it. Her eyes widened with terror as Jabez came out of the shadows. Before she could scream, he seized her and clasped a huge hand over her mouth, covering her nostrils so she could not breathe. The grave robber's trick, she thought before she lost consciousness.

When she came to, she was slung over the giant's shoulder like a sack of flour and being carried through the wet darkness. She screamed out and tried to get away from him. But her screams went unheard and her efforts to escape were met with cruel hands that held her tightly.

Ahead the old castle loomed in the stormy night. And now Jabez went down a stone flight of steps to a wooden door which he hurled open. The door opened on a long, dark stone-lined tunnel so low that the monster had to lower his head as he dragged her along. She was sobbing and pleading with him to let her go.

She might as well have spoken to the wind. He paid no attention to her. The tunnel seemed endless. After a long while they came to a second wooden door. This one led to another flight of stone steps, which she thought would bring them to the ground floor of the castle, but she was too terrified and confused to be sure about anything.

She knew that the old castle had been built by a wealthy Boston man who tired of it and had not lived there for years. It had the smell of a place long deserted and neglected. Much of it was in ruin when she'd first seen it, but she supposed Bentley didn't mind this. The castle was vast and there would still be plenty of room in repair for the use of him and his followers.

Jabez half-carried, half-dragged her along a hallway until he came to an arched door with ornamental wood carvings on it. He shoved it and took her inside, into a dark room. He let her drop on the cold stone floor and then went out, slamming and locking the door after him.

She crouched there shivering from fear and the chill of the damp floor. She had no idea what area of the castle she was in or what would happen to her next. She could only pray that John Williams might find she'd disappeared and spread the alarm. She was sure either Barnabas or Quentin would quickly come to her rescue. But at this moment they supposed her safely in bed at Collinwood.

A horrible, high-pitched scream came from the corridor and hung in the air for long chilling seconds. She stopped her ears with her fingers to shut out its anguish. After a moment she took her fingers away and there was only silence again.

What had the scream meant? Had it signified the death of some innocent at the evil Nicholas Bentley's hands? Or had it been the cry of a lost soul, a phantom whom the vile doctor was bending to his will? It might even have been a scream from some participant in a black mass. Whatever it had been, it was typical of the awful menace of this place!

She thought she heard footsteps coming slowly along the

corridor. Fear rose more strongly in her. She stood and braced herself against the stone wall of the prison-like chamber. There was the grating of a key in the rusty lock and then the door swung open.

Nicholas Bentley appeared in the doorway, holding a flaming torch in his hand. For a moment she hardly recognized him. The suave surgeon had degenerated into a madman with a beard-stubbled countenance and wild eyes. His clothing was dirty and disheveled, and his hair was in wild disarray.

"I don't imagine you were expecting to see me, Miss Sullivan," he began. At least his voice sounded the same.

"You're mad to do this!"

He took a step further into the dark room with the torch held high. "You look as beautiful as ever when you're angry," he complimented her with a sneering smile.

"This is not London," she warned him. "You'll soon find yourself in trouble here."

"But I also had trouble in London, thanks to you and your precious father," he said nastily. "Well, I settled with him and John Williams. Now it is your turn."

She pretended a bravery she didn't feel. "You daren't harm me."

Bentley chuckled, sending a chill along her spine. "I have no thought of harming you as yet," he said. "I'm still hoping you may decide to be my wife. You would be charming presiding at the castle table."

"Stop making fun of me," she protested.

"I'm serious," he said. "And you should realize that, since I've followed you across half the world."

"That only proves you to be insane."

"You have found new friends in Collinsport," the evil doctor said. "But I know how to manage them. It won't take me long to discredit your friend Barnabas."

"You can't harm him!" she declared defiantly.

A smirk crossed his jaundiced face. "We'll find out about that." As he spoke, a shadow appeared in the hallway behind him. He turned and called out, "It's all right, Lily. You can join us."

Cold terror surged through Paula again as Lily came sauntering into the room. The painted face and the arrogant smile were the same, but she was wearing a rich brown silk dress trimmed with golden lace. It was a formal dress of ancient vintage… something she'd found in the old castle, perhaps.

"Hello, luv!" she said in her familiar way.

"You see that Lily has made the journey with me," Dr. Bentley said, with the torch held to highlight the painted face of the living dead woman.

"Please," Paula begged. "Let me go!"

He laughed. "Now it is you who must be joking. Lily is going to help our cause by incriminating your friend Barnabas. When he was last in Collinsport his needs forced him to attack a number of the young women of the village and drink their blood."

Lily smiled. "Me and Barnabas roamed London together many a night."

"Of course you did," the doctor encouraged her. "And this time Barnabas has been careful to make forays to other neighboring places for his victims, so as not to cause a sensation. But Lily will change that. Beginning tonight she will go to the village and find soft throats to quench her thirst." He turned to the vampire. "Isn't that right, Lily?"

She closed her eyes in a dreamy fashion. "Velvet throats!" she murmured. "Young throats of velvet!"

"That's the way it will be, Lily," Bentley said with a leering approval. And he told Paula, "You see how well it is going to work out. Lily will sink her fangs in the throats of the village maidens and Barnabas will be blamed."

She knew that the scheme would almost certainly work. It was all too likely the villagers would turn on Barnabas, since he had been involved in such happenings before. And she began to worry about him as much as herself. If there was only some way to get out and warn him.

She said, "Whatever happens to Barnabas you'll still have Quentin to reckon with!"

Dr. Bentley smiled derisively. "The werewolf?"

"I'm not telling you anything," she said.

"You don't have to," he assured her. "I know everything about the Collins family. Their long history of ghosts in the old mansion, the legends of the werewolf and the vampire, the phantom mariner and all the rest. And if Quentin attempts to interfere with me, I'll find a way to deal with him."

Lily told her, "Better come over to our side, luv." She eyed the woman with disgust.

"I'd rather die."

"An interesting suggestion," Bentley said, pouncing on her words. "You see, dying could be your first step in joining my company of friends. You haven't met them yet, but you will. After your death I have only to prepare your body with my serum and you then become truly useful to me."

"You wouldn't dare try anything like that," she said, but it was all bravado. She knew that he was mad enough to attempt anything.

"My experiment has proven a success," the madman said. "I can now produce the same results with my serum the voodoo doctors do with their witchcraft. I can manufacture zombies at will."

Lily said, "It's the truth, luv. I've seen him at it."

The doctor gave her a distasteful look. "Time to be on your way, Lily. You can go to the village at once. And the more throats you find the better."

The painted face took on a dreadful smile. "Just like London again," she said in a hoarse whisper. And she vanished into the shadows of the corridor.

Bentley smiled at Paula. "You must admit I planned that well. At first it seemed too much bother to bring Lily with us. Then I decided I could make good use of her. And what better use than to get Barnabas in trouble."

"They'll see her. They'll know it's not Barnabas!"

He shook his head. "Not Lily. They'll never set eyes on her. She mingles with the shadows and then when her teeth are on the throats of the innocent, it is too late." She knew it was probably true; the victims would be so confused they wouldn't know who had attacked them and Barnabas would be the logical suspect.

She said, "You'll be trapped by your own evil one day soon. You can't go on this way."

"You're thinking of the serpent who sinks its poison fangs into itself," he said. "I promise you I won't oblige. And now I'm going to ask you to come with me." Paula shrank back.

"No!"

"But you must! I have a surprise for you!"

There was a mysterious gloating in his voice, a menace which she knew was there but didn't understand. "You can't make me go!"

"Perhaps not," he said calmly. "But I have only to summon Jabez and he will see that you obey. It would be easier for you if I didn't have to do that."

She saw that further refusal was useless. In a dull voice, she asked, "Where are you taking me?"

The torch still in one hand, he used the other to take her arm and lead her out to the corridor. "You are going to see the success of my experiment," he said. "We are going downstairs to the dungeon of the zombies."

CHAPTER 11

The very words chilled her to the marrow. More than ever now, she was convinced that Bentley had lost his mind. Both his appearance and his talk indicated that he'd deteriorated mentally and physically since his days as one of London's leading surgeons.

She attempted to pull away from him, but his grip was strong. And even if she should manage to escape, it would not be for long in the crumbling mansion. Jabez knew the maze of corridors much better than she did and so would have no difficulty blocking her way to freedom.

He led her into a large room with a vaulted ceiling which might have been a banquet hall at one time. Tapestries hung from the walls and he pushed one of these aside and pressed on a wood panel. At once a secret door opened to reveal a black passageway.

Holding the torch he nodded for her to enter the secret door. "You go first."

She made no reply. It seemed there wasn't any point. Anything she said would only upset him further. Filled with apprehension, she entered the damp, dark passage and as her eyes became accustomed to it she saw that it led to a spiral stone stairway winding around in a narrow stone-lined area.

"Go on," Bentley said harshly.

"I can't see," she said in an effort to waste time.

He shoved the torch forward to light the way. "You can see well enough," he said. "Don't pretend!"

So she started down the steep, winding stone steps, touching a hand to the damp circular wall to keep her balance. The mad doctor came closely behind her. They went down far enough for her to believe they were descending to the cellars.

Apprehensively she glanced back over her shoulder. "Where are you taking me?"

He smiled that frightening cruel smile of his. "I told you. The dungeon of the zombies. It is important that they have a place well removed from the rest of the house, where they will not be seen by ordinary visitors. I'm sure you understand."

Trembling, she halted on the stairs to say, "I understand nothing of this. I don't want to see the product of your experiments. It all sickens and terrifies me!"

His burning eyes fixed on her as he stood above her on the steps with the blazing torch breaking the shadowed gloom. "I like your spirit," he said. "You're a fool not to consider marriage with me."

"You shouldn't dare suggest such a thing, after what you did to my father!" she said bitterly.

"Your father was an idiot and got what he deserved!"

"And so shall you," she warned him.

He used the torch as a prod to threaten her. "On down!"

They went a further few twists of the spiral stairway and then came to another corridor with a rounded brick roof and brick walls. He forced her along it until they came to a heavy plank door with a padlock on it. He produced a worn iron key and inserted it in the lock, which opened with a creaking protest.

With a grin on his beard-stubbled face, he removed the padlock and told her, "Now you will see." He opened the door to reveal a room almost completely in darkness except for a flickering candle on a long wooden table.

And then she saw the faces! The blank, expressionless faces staring at her with unseeing eyes. There were seven or eight in the room, a mixture of men and women, most of them elderly. Their clothes were shabby and their faces lined and pale.

Dr. Bentley moved among them, saying, "I have brought a visitor to show you off, to prove how fully my experiments have been tested. You needn't move or make any fuss. Just allow her to study you and appreciate the miracle you represent."

The sorry figures in the dark cellar room obeyed him. They stood there with their faces all turned her way, but not seeming to be looking at her. Like Jabez they were as silent as the dead.

He turned to her triumphantly. "Had ever a man such servants?"

She was terrified. "I don't know what you've done to them," she said. "You've made them mutilated victims of your lust for power. Mindless robots!"

"They are better off than in the grave where I found them."

"I disagree. Death is their natural condition. You are robbing them of that!"

"These people act on my command," he said, "and only on my command. I plan to have an army of them. And then I shall take over the earth. I shall be the master of the dead and the living will obey my dictates."

"You are mad."

"If so, it is the madness of genius," Bentley told her. "And I'm not ashamed of that. Now I'm going to leave you here alone with these creatures for a little. It may mellow you and make you appreciate me more when I return."

Panic filled her at the thought of being left in the dungeon with the dead. "No," she cried, running up to him. "You wouldn't!"

He thrust the torch at her to keep her back. "I have made my decision," he said. "You must be taught a lesson." And to the zombies clustered at the other end of the room, he ordered, "Watch over this young woman. Get to know her so that you will recognize her if you encounter her again." And having said this, he quickly withdrew from the dungeon and closed and locked the door.

She ran to the door and screamed, "Please! Don't leave me here!" She was sobbing and shaking with fear, her hands pressed against the planks of the door.

She felt a cold, limp hand on her shoulder and wheeled around, her pretty face distorted with terror, to confront a bent old man with an emaciated face and toothless gums. His long gray hair had grown until it almost reached his shoulders and his nose was hooked. His staring eyes seemed never to fix directly on her, but she knew he was giving her a close study.

"Go away!" she sobbed.

But he paid no attention to her; his orders had come from Dr. Nicholas Bentley. Again he reached out to touch her arm tentatively. At the same time the ragged band from the other end of the room crept through the shadows like sleepwalkers to cluster around her. Not a sound escaped their lips, but they kept silently moving nearer her until she thought she would suffocate from the odor of decay which hung over them.

She edged along the wall and they followed her, so close they almost pressed against her body. She sobbed dryly and kept in motion. Then she saw the few sticks on the floor and an idea was born out of her desperation.

Swooping to the floor, she quickly picked up two thin sticks and held them up in front of her in the shape of a cross. It had an immediate effect. With a chorus of weird moans, the zombies faltered and awkwardly stumbled back.

"The cross!" she cried. "The cross your master has so defiled!" And she kept the makeshift cross in front of her.

The zombies kept drawing back until they were the ones crouched silently in the distant shadows. At least they presented no immediate threat to her, but the candle on the plank table was almost burned out. When its light failed, she'd be left in darkness with the phantom creatures. Meanwhile she remained against the door with the makeshift cross in her hands in a state of siege.

She did not know how long she was there. The flame of the candle was flickering in a limpid pool of wax. Perhaps in minutes it would go out. And what then?

At that moment the door was unlocked and Dr. Bentley entered again. He saw the makeshift cross and the cowering zombies and his reaction was a soft laugh. She was surprised.

"You are intelligent," he commended her. "The kind of wife I could admire. Too good material to be reduced to one of these." He waved to the zombies.

"All I ask is to be allowed to leave," she said weakly. "I have endured your torture. Isn't that enough to satisfy you?"

"Not quite," he said. "I want you with me. At my side."

"Never!"

"All you need is time to think it over," he assured her. "The alternative is my operating room. That and a ritual ceremony will send you down here to spend your days with these creatures."

"No!" she pleaded.

"Either remain here a mindless creature eager to do my bidding, confined to the dungeon until I need you, or enjoy all the power I've come to possess. You can sit at my side like a queen!"

"Barnabas will have something to say about that!"

His smile was cold. "I can tell you need proper time for thought. No need to rush things." And he seized her by the arm and took her out of the dungeon.

The tortuous journey up the winding spiral stairway took them to the upper level of the castle, and one of the tower rooms. It was a small, dust-ridden cubicle with a narrow barred window looking out over the bay. There was a wooden table and a chair in the center of it and some blankets on the floor.

He thrust her into the tiny chamber and told her, "It is not furnished as you are used to, but it will give you an excellent background for thought. By the time I return I trust you will have changed your mind."

"Never!" she said firmly, despite her weariness and fear.

"Then I have explained what will happen."

He locked the door and left her there. It was damp and cool and the blankets were filthy. But she lay on the floor with them wrapped around her, deciding that she was at least better off than she'd been in the dungeon with those mindless things. What had Bentley done to them? Were they truly lost souls stolen from their graves and restored to this weird semblance of life?

It frightened her to think about it, to know that such things existed. And they were so near, in the cellar of the castle. Finally through sheer exhaustion she fell into a deep sleep.

The sound of the key being turned in the door lock wakened her. She sat up quickly, not fully awake, and watched the door slowly open as Jabez came in bearing a tray with food. He placed it silently on the table and turned and left.

In spite of her dreadful predicament she found herself hungry and ready to eat. The food was simple but good enough. When she finished she began to pace restlessly up and down. She went to the barred window, which had a view of the bay and a bare glimpse of Collinwood to the left. The sight of it made her wonder about what was happening there.

Surely she had been missed by this time. And though Barnabas would not know about it until he awakened at dusk, there was some hope that Quentin would find out sooner. And Quentin was truly a man of action. John Williams, too, would surely try to do something for her. It seemed to add up to a matter of waiting and hoping for outside aid.

Could she prevail against Dr. Bentley in the meantime? She could only hope so. He seemed ready to let her alone for a little and that was something to be thankful for. She was still standing grasping the bars of the slit of a window and staring out when Jabez returned to get her empty dishes.

Then he summoned her with a wave of his hand. She was not a little frightened as to what this might mean, but she felt she had no choice but to do as he indicated. She went out into the corridor and he herded her along until they reached a grated door. Then he opened this and let her step out in the fresh air and sunshine of the roof. After that he stood guard by the door.

Now she understood. She was to have a brief period to enjoy the air and warm sun of the tower roof. Then she would be returned to her cell-like room to await Nicholas Bentley. At least she could be grateful for the small privilege. It was better than languishing in the confined quarters of the room she'd been imprisoned in.

Moving to the edge, as far away from the door as she could, she took stock of the area and tried to find some means of escape. Apparently there were none, unless she took the drastic measure of leaping over the side to the ground so far below that it looked like a toy world. Just peering down made her dizzy.

She moved across to the left of the tower roof to get a good look at Collinwood. Even up here and so far distant it had a solid appearance. It was a large, rambling building, whole sections of it not being in use. Further on were the group of buildings loosely called the stables and still beyond them the old house in which Barnabas was staying. She could even see the sloping field below the old house and the Collins family cemetery at the bottom of it.

She was taking in all this magnificent view when she heard someone moving behind her. She turned and almost cried out when she found herself staring at John Williams. The young doctor quickly placed a finger to his lips to warn her to silence and nodded toward the door where Jabez waited. Then he signaled her to join him in a spot hidden from the door by a chimney.

Paula hurried to him in the sheltering ell of the chimney and said, "I couldn't believe it was you. How did you get here?"

"There's a secret passage," he said. "I stumbled on it by accident."

She asked tensely, "What is going on at Collinwood?"

"There's a great to-do about your being missing," John said with a grim look. "I knew at once you'd be here and I came over and began searching for a way to get in. I was lucky in finding a passage that led up here."

"I've only been here a short time," she said. "And he'll be taking me back to the room soon. If you hadn't come now you'd have missed me. Does Quentin know what has happened?"

"I don't expect so. He hasn't been near Collinwood."

"Someone should tell him," she worried. "And Barnabas also, when he wakens."

"I can do that."

She stared at him. "Why can't I leave with you now?"

A muscle in his cheek twitched nervously. "Too risky," he said. "I don't dare try to take you down the passage. We're too likely to be caught in the daylight."

She gazed anxiously toward the barred door behind which Jabez waited, seemingly unaware of John Williams' presence.

In a tense whisper, she asked, "Isn't it worth a try?"

The haggard face showed fear. "You know what Bentley is like. If he caught us, the reprisals would be twice as severe as anything we've known yet. Better to wait until after dark."

"When Barnabas and Quentin can help you?"

"Yes."

"I suppose it is the best plan," she agreed reluctantly. "But I'm in terrible danger here every minute that passes."

"You've managed so far."

"You have no idea what I've been through," she warned him. And she thought how different he was from the John Williams she'd once known. The mad doctor had broken his spirit to the point where he was almost like the zombies in the cellar.

There was a haunted gleam in John's eyes. "I know what it can be like. I was his prisoner once, remember? And he never did set Jane free. He murdered her!"

She touched a restraining hand on his arm. "Don't think about it."

"But don't worry," he said. "It will only be a matter of a few hours until I return with a rescue expedition."

"I've prayed for that."

"It will come," he promised. "Let me get the others around me so there will be no mistakes."

Paula eyed him anxiously. She whispered, "You used to be so brave!"

The hollow eyes looked hurt. "I risked coming up here to you, didn't I?"

She knew this was so and she regretted hurting him. "I'm sorry," she said.

"It doesn't matter," he told her. "Now I must leave you and hurry back to Collinwood."

"Don't be seen," she warned him.

He looked grim. "If I am, it's the finish for me."

"I'll go back to Jabez and keep his attention."

"Good!" The haggard young doctor took her in his arms for a brief kiss. "That will have to do until I return for you. Courage!"

He moved back behind the chimney and vanished almost as quickly as he'd appeared. She had no real conception of where the secret door to the roof was, but she was thankful he'd found it and come to her.

Now she must play her part and trust that she would be safe until he returned. She went to the door and opened it. Jabez waited there impassively; his manner told her that he had seen and heard nothing.

She told him, "I want to return to my room."

He led the way, and when she reached it he locked her in again. It would be hours until nightfall and she worried that Dr. Bentley would come to her again. She wouldn't be able to make him wait longer for her decision.

Paging up and down the rough plank floor filled in some of the time. When she was thoroughly exhausted, she stretched out on the pile of rags that passed for blankets. She was there when the door opened late in the afternoon and Bentley entered, thin and menacing. He had shaven since she'd seen him last and the hawk-face was more as of old.

But the mad light in his eyes was as strong as ever.

"Well," he said in his harsh voice, "have you had plenty of hours to think?"

She had gotten to her feet. "I've been too confused to make decisions."

"Really?" His tone was sarcastic.

The sinking sun was sending its warm amber rays through the barred window; perhaps within two or three hours her rescuers led by an awakened Barnabas would arrive.

She told the mad doctor, "Give me more time."

"I don't consider that it is necessary."

"Please!" she begged.

His smile was taunting. "You're hoping that by waiting you'll be rescued. You're expecting Barnabas, aren't you?"

She was frightened by his words but tried hard to cover her fear. "Why do you say that?"

"I know it's true," he snapped. "Let me warn you. Don't expect Barnabas!"

She stared at him. "Has something happened to him?"

Bentley nodded. "Lily did her work exceedingly well. Not only did she taste the blood from two of the village girls last night, she completely drained the body of a third one. And so now she will have a new associate."

Paula's eyes widened in horror. "No!"

He nodded. "She made an interesting choice for her victim. The vicar's daughter. She will be buried tomorrow. And tomorrow night we will rescue her body from the grave and she will join us here."

"Barnabas and Quentin won't let you!"

"Barnabas is being blamed for the crime," Bentley said with relish. "He is probably a prisoner in the jailhouse at this very moment. Quentin won't venture here without him," the doctor predicted. "It is Barnabas who has the real courage. Quentin always follows."

"What about John Williams?" she said. "You're forgetting him!"

"Williams has been half-mad since I held him captive and sent his wife to the hospital dissecting table," Bentley said with a sneer. "So you have no one to count on."

"You sound very sure of that," she said with despair in her voice. "I am."

"I'll still say what I've told you before. I don't want anything to do with you!" It was the defiance of complete distress. She'd really given up.

He eyed her coldly. "You mean that?"

"I do."

"You won't become my wife?"

"No."

"Very well," he said with a new quietness in his voice that worried her more than ever. "Then there is nothing to do but make the preparations."

"What preparations?"

"For you to become one of the mindless ones. I warned you!"

"No!" She stepped back.

His smile was pure evil. "Perhaps it is better this way. As one of my zombies, you will make a more docile wife. I'm really coming to prefer the company of the dead to the living."

"You're despicable!"

"You will find it quite a painless process," he assured her. "We begin by having a brief voodoo ceremony, an excursion into black magic, really. And then I open an artery and drain your blood."

She pressed her hands to her ears. "I don't want to know!"

"I think you should," he went on. "And when your body is empty of the precious red liquid I fill it with a pink serum of my own making. You'll notice the skins of those in the dungeon are strangely pale. It is because of the color of the serum. And then you are allowed to rest for some hours. When you wake you wholly belong to me."

"I'll never belong to you."

"Don't say such nonsensical things," he told her coolly. "I could have done this to you when you first came last night. Only my tolerance has given these extra hours. But it seems you don't properly appreciate my kind nature."

"You are vicious and cruel," she cried. "A king of grave robbers!"

"I rather like the title," he said, looking grimly amused. "It does fit me, doesn't it? And when the time comes and all the furore has died down I'll take you back to London with me."

"You'd never dare set foot in England again," she challenged him. "The police would be hot on your trail."

"The police are inclined to forget after a few years," the doctor said. "And with you as my wife I'll call at Widenham Square and we'll take over the mansion. Your Aunt Lucy will be too senile to care one way or the other by then."

She knew it could happen. She tried to think of herself as one of those silent, staring creatures in the darkness of the dungeon. She should have flung herself from the tower when she'd had the chance.

Bentley bowed with mock politeness. "Now I'll leave you to some last thoughts. And if they should be of Barnabas I warn you they're wasted. Barnabas is as good as dead. The authorities will take care of him for what happened last night."

"You're lying!" she cried as he turned to leave.

He smiled over his shoulder. "Believe me, I'm not." He went on out and locked the plank door.

If it had been bad before for her it was much worse now. She couldn't think of anything but the trouble Barnabas must be in, and the fate that was so shortly awaiting her. She no longer had any doubts that Bentley meant what he said—she was about to become one of his prize exhibits.

She went to the window and stared out at the bay. Again she regretted that she hadn't thrown herself to her death from the tower roof when she'd had the opportunity. Now it was too late.

But the appearance of John Williams up there had bolstered her hopes. He'd promised to return, and she'd believed him. Yet somehow he didn't seem to realize the hazard. And he hadn't said anything about the vampire attacks or Barnabas being blamed for them.

Surely he would have said something if they had taken place. This thought restored a little of her courage. Perhaps the evil doctor had been lying after all, and none of the things he'd said about Barnabas were true. But even at that, it was hardly likely her rescuers would arrive before he had robbed her of her mind and any hope of a normal life.

She slumped into the plain chair and sobbed. She was still seated there as dusk arrived and the room became full of shadows. She had no candle to light and so she sat in the near darkness, staring ahead in stark terror and waiting.

The key grated in the door and it opened. Lily, carrying a giant silver goblet, came sauntering into the room.

"Something for you, luv!"

She was on her feet. "I don't want it."

"Better be smart. It's wine. You may wish you'd taken it before this night is over." The vampire offered the goblet to her.

"It's poisoned or contains some awful drug," she said, backing away.

"No, luv! It's pure wine! I tasted it myself, though it's not what I like best," Lily said with a leer.

"What about last night?" Paula asked her.

"Last night?"

"Did you attack some village girls and turn one into a vampire?"

Lily smiled to herself. "I had me a bit of fun. I don't remember it all. After the first one I was like drunk, you see."

"But you did go into the village and attack some girls?"

"Of course, luv," Lily said with mild surprise. "Didn't the doctor say I could?"

Paula turned away from her, filled with loathing. It seemed that Bentley hadn't lied. Barnabas was in a dreadful predicament. Had the villagers already driven the stake through his heart?

CHAPTER 12

She was standing there in despair at Lily's news when Bentley appeared in the doorway with Jabez at his side. She knew it was the signal for her removal to whatever dire fate awaited her.

"You haven't taken the wine," Bentley said, glancing at the goblet on the plank table.

"No," Paula said. "I don't want it."

"You may need it," he warned her.

"I prefer not to touch it."

Bentley shrugged. "As you wish. We are now going to proceed to the ceremonial hall and begin our ritual. Lily and Jabez will be your attendants. I will act as the High Priest."

"Suppose I refuse to leave this room?"

He smiled dourly. "In that case Jabez will remove you by force. And I think having experienced his not-too-tender handling you would prefer to go quietly."

She said nothing as he stood aside for her to go. It seemed to her there was nothing else she could do. She looked at the threatening trio—Bentley with his cruel smile, Jabez stolid and staring blankly ahead of him, and Lily watching her tensely.

It was Lily who offered the only word of encouragement. "Don't mind, luv. It won't be so bad. And it will soon be over with."

Nicholas Bentley gave the vampire a sharp glance. "She can

manage very well without your encouragement, Lily!"

"No offense, Doctor," the woman said hastily.

Bentley took Paula by the arm. "Come along. I want to get the ceremony under way. The operation afterward is a trying one and I prefer not to be too tired when I begin it."

Her heart was pounding with fear. She allowed him to lead her out into the dark hallway and down the stairs to the lower level of the castle. The room to which he took her was a huge one at the rear of the castle, with windows on a balcony facing the cliffs. There was a sheer drop down the face of the cliff from the balcony and she began to plan how she could break away and reach the balcony. It would only take her seconds to plunge over the side to her death on the sea-washed rocks far below.

And she would finally be free. The ordeal of the past long months would have come to an end. Perhaps somewhere in that world on the other side she would be able to reach out and join hands with Barnabas. She had to believe that. It was her only hope.

Bentley halted half-way along the length of the great ceremonial hall. "Unique, isn't it? Truly like one of the ancient castles. And ideal for our purpose."

She was taking everything in with dull eyes. The windows of the room were draped in red velvet and at the far end was a table on a raised platform, with red velvet drapes along the whole length of the wall behind it. In stands at either side of the table, torches burned. These supplied the only light in the great room.

Bentley said, "We will proceed to the dais." And he led her up there with Jabez and Lily silently following. When they reached the platform he had her step up on it and stand facing the table. Lily and Jabez took positions looking up at her from either side of the flaming torches. Bentley was beside her.

"I will now put on the ceremonial robes," he said. Reaching beneath the table, he drew out a long, flowing black robe and a crimson skull cap. After he had donned these he raised a hand over her head and said some words in a tongue unknown to her. His burning eyes seemed brighter than ever.

Then gazing at her with a strange intentness he said, "Lie down on the table."

She gave him a final pleading look. "Please!" It was a last appeal.

"Too late to change our plans now," he said. And he firmly assisted her to stretch out on the table.

Paula lay there staring up at the ceiling with its decorated plaster work. She was waiting for what would happen next and measuring the distance to the side windows with their balconies. If she could reach one of them without any of the three stopping her, she could quickly end her life.

Bentley was intoning strange words over her again. And then he reached under the table and produced a long thin-bladed knife which he held high over her. It was completely unexpected and sent new terror racing through her.

He lit an incense burner and continued murmuring those strange words as the incense wafted upward. It had a weird, sweet smell which at once made her feel ill and her head reel. She began to think it had some strange, secret ingredient in it which was acting like a drug on her. She feared it would make her unconscious and she would not be able to carry through her escape plan.

Bentley cut the air with the sharp-bladed knife and then carefully touched its keen edge to her throat. For one awful moment she thought he was going to plunge it into her throat but instead he lifted it again.

At that very instant a door slammed and she heard footsteps running into the room. Bentley gasped and she turned her head to see Barnabas in his caped coat and Quentin in his flowing black cloak. Barnabas had his sword cane unsheathed and was marching towards Bentley with a grim look on his handsome, gaunt face.

Bentley shouted, "Get him, Jabez!"

But Quentin had already thrown himself on the huge brown man and they were struggling wildly on the floor. With a scream, Lily turned and raced from the room. Bentley backed away from the table to the rear of the platform and Paula jumped from the table and went down to Barnabas.

Barnabas waved her aside. "Over there!"

Bentley had backed to the wall and was pressed against the broad red velvet drapes, a bizarre figure in the black robe and red skull cap. "Keep away from me, Barnabas!" he shouted, his voice echoing in the great empty room.

"We're finally going to settle accounts, Bentley," Barnabas said, approaching the evil doctor with his sword bared.

On the floor Quentin and the zombie were having what could well be a life and death struggle. Standing a distance away Paula was shocked by the savage battle between them.

Bentley was edging along the wall, his hands upraised. "Keep away from me, Collins. You have no quarrel with me!"

"I disagree," Barnabas said in a low menacing voice. And he suddenly sprang at the mad doctor and plunged his sword into his side. He drew the weapon out stained with blood. Bentley screamed and clutched at the wound, then ran from the platform toward one of the balcony windows.

"No!" Bentley screamed in abject fear, holding onto his side, the red skull cap falling from his head and the robe flowing after him. He staggered to the balcony door and flung it open.

"It's time, Bentley!" Barnabas cried, and as the madman reached the balcony he sank the full length of his sword blade in him.

Bentley gave a great moaning cry, and with his hands high above him, stumbled over to the railing and then plummeted backward. He vanished over the side to crash down on the rocks hundreds of feet below. The dark career of Dr. Nicholas Bentley had finally ended.

Paula turned away with a glimpse of Barnabas standing on the balcony, sword still in hand, and staring down after the body. Now she was confronted by the still bitter struggle between Quentin and Jabez. As they rolled over, they upset one of the stands holding the torch. It fell backward, touching a velvet curtain that caught fire immediately.

"Barnabas!" Paula screamed.

At the same instant a weird transformation took place on the floor where the struggle was going on. Quentin seemed to change in face and figure and in place of the good-looking young man, there was a grotesque stranger with the hairy hand of an animal and the features of a wolf. With a snarl this creature tore at the throat of the powerful Jabez and ripped it open. Blood spurted forth and Jabez ceased struggling.

She turned from the awful sight as the fire went on raging from the velvet curtains to other objects in the huge room. The smoke was blinding and choking. Barnabas came and took her by the arm.

"The fire has a headway here. Nothing we can do," he said.

As they started out of the room, she gazed back into the billowing clouds of smoke. "What about Quentin?" she cried.

"He'll make out," Barnabas said. They rushed from the room and down a stairway to the main entrance hall.

A moment later Quentin came bounding down the stairs to join them. He was disheveled and pale as he said, "That's the end of those two."

"There are others," she said. "Lily, the vampire and those zombies he created in a dungeon off the cellar."

"Can you show the way?" Barnabas asked.

"Yes."

They followed as she led them down into the cellar. The smoke had already started to seep down there and the heat from the burning castle above them was intense. In spite of its stone work there was much wood in its construction and apparently it had been as dry as tinder. The flames were racing from floor to floor and the smoke was dangerously thick everywhere.

Paula's eyes smarted and she coughed as she paused to consider the maze of corridors. It was important that she find the right one. "Down this way," she decided at last.

Barnabas was close behind her. "We daren't stay in here long," he warned. "The building above may collapse at any time."

"I agree," Quentin coughed. "Those things will be destroyed in the fire anyway. No need to try finding them."

Paula leaned against the wall and held a hankie over her mouth as she tried to breathe. "We'll have to go back."

And they did. On their way, they stumbled over the prostrate body of an unconscious Lily. Barnabas lifted her up in his arms and carried her to a side door of the cellar which led to the open. He deposited her on the grass. Paula and Quentin were beside him. They all looked at the flaming castle with awed eyes.

"Did you ever see such a sight?" Barnabas said.

"The flames will be visible in Collinsport," Quentin guessed.

"Some of the Collinwood people will be here soon," Barnabas said worriedly. And glancing down at the stretched out figure of Lily, he went on, "We've got to make a decision about her."

Paula looked at him with frightened eyes. "What will you do?"

"Take her back in there," Quentin said, disgust on his good-looking face. "She's a threat to herself and everyone else."

Barnabas' gaunt face was highlighted by the crimson reflection of the burning building behind them as he gave Quentin a reproachful look. "You should know better than that!"

"What do you mean?" Quentin asked.

"The flames won't kill her," Barnabas said with meaning.

"That's true," Quentin said, as if he were suddenly remembering. "There's only one way to destroy her."

"Have we a right?" Barnabas asked.

"We have a duty," Quentin said solemnly. "You know the harm she did last night. Crimes for which you were blamed."

Barnabas looked down grimly at the motionless figure of Lily. "And she will do it again," he agreed quietly.

"You wait here," Quentin said. "I'll be back in a moment."

Paula watched him hurry off toward the yard at the other end of the burning castle. She gave Barnabas a frightened look. "What is he going to do?"

"You'll see," Barnabas said tautly. His eyes stared up at the towering flames rising above the turrets of the quickly-burning castle. "This will mark the end of the castle. It's walls will crumble soon."

"Those poor mutilated creatures in the cellar dungeon must have suffocated by now," she said in a tone of distress.

"At least it ended their thralldom to Bentley."

Her eyes met his. "You finally made him pay."

"It was past time."

Quentin came hurrying back. "I found some wood and an axe," he said. "We have what we need."

Paula stared at the pointed stake he was carrying in one hand and the axe he had in the other. "What are you going to do?"

Barnabas said. "It would be better if you turned your back."

"Yes," Quentin said in a tense voice.

"Poor Lily!" she cried in distress.

"We have no choice," Barnabas said with a sigh and he gently turned Paula so her back was to the burning building and the outstretched body of Lily on the grass.

She clenched her hands and waited. She heard the sound of the axe striking the stake. Pounding it. And then there was an eerie, high-pitched wailing from Lily which lasted for seconds before it trailed off. She slowly turned and saw the two men staring down at Lily's body. The stake had been driven through her heart.

"Barnabas!" Paula went close to him so that he would comfort her in his arms.

Quentin spoke urgently behind her. "It would be best to take the body back inside. Let the flames destroy it now."

"Be careful going in there," Barnabas warned him.

"I know what I'm doing," Quentin said with a touch of his old reckless manner. And he lifted the body with the stake driven through it and began carrying it back to the burning building.

Paula had turned to watch and now she cried, "He'll be burned to death."

"I think not," Barnabas said. "He is only going to set the body inside the entrance."

She watched as Quentin entered the flaming castle. He vanished and she felt sure he was gone for good. But within seconds he dodged back and came hurrying across the lawn to join them. He smelled of smoke but he was unharmed.

"The walls are ready to go," he warned them. "We should stand back a distance."

"I agree," Barnabas said and he hustled Paula backward with him.

They had barely gotten out of the way when one of the towers and upper walls came melting down with a shower of great stones. And quickly on the heels of this, another section of the castle collapsed. The roar of the flames and the crackling of the wood filled the air.

Quentin gazed at the flames. "Well, that's the end of the threat. All of them are dead."

Barnabas looked doubtful. "I'm not so sure."

"Why do you say that?" Paula asked.

"There are certain things I do not understand," Barnabas said. "But time enough to find out the answers later."

"I say that Bentley and his crew of grave robbers have all been taken care of," Quentin said irascibly. "I don't understand why you say different."

Paula didn't like to see them arguing. She said, "I assume John

Williams told you where I was?"

Barnabas frowned. "John Williams?"

"Yes. He managed to get to me in the castle this afternoon. But he was afraid to try and rescue me on his own. He left me to go back and enlist the aid of you two."

"It's the first I've heard about it," Barnabas said.

"And I," Quentin said. "And I talked with him late this afternoon."

"He must have been too terrified to tell you about me," she worried. "Bentley broke him completely. He was very afraid of Bentley, even though he hated him."

"I gathered that," Barnabas agreed.

"How did you know where to find me?" Paula asked.

"It wasn't hard to guess you'd been abducted here," Barnabas said.

"And so we came to your rescue," Quentin said with a wry smile.

"You were both wonderful," she told them.

Quentin gave her a wise look. "I'm through," he said. "You're out of danger as far as I'm concerned. Barnabas may have other ideas, but I say he's wrong. And so I'm going on my way."

She stared at him. "You're leaving?"

"Yes."

"Right now?"

He nodded. "I'm going to the village and get my things. I'll be gone by the morning. There'll be a lot of talk and I'd just as soon not have to be around here to explain to the authorities."

Barnabas looked grim. "You have a right to go when you like. But I still doubt that the danger is fully over."

Quentin smiled in his bitter way. "Then you protect her from whatever it is." He turned to her. "Goodbye, Paula. I know it's Barnabas you love and that's another reason for my going."

Her eyes met his in a gentle look. "I'm sorry, Quentin. And I am so grateful to you."

"I was happy to be able to do something for you," he said. And with that he drew her to him and touched his lips to hers. Then he let her go and winked at Barnabas. "A kiss I've stolen from you, Cousin Barnabas."

Barnabas smiled. "You are most welcome. Be careful when you reach the village."

"I understand," Quentin said. And he turned and walked away into the darkness.

She felt the full weight of his loss almost at once. A heavy sadness came over her. To try and rid herself of it, she turned her eyes to the blazing castle again. It was still shooting flames and smoke mixed with sparks high in the dark sky.

Barnabas touched her arm. "I see some of the folk from Collinwood arriving. More will turn up shortly. I don't think we should be here. They could ask some awkward questions."

She gave him an anxious glance. "Then we should slip away?"

"Yes," he said, taking her arm and guiding her off to the right. They kept close to the clouds of smoke so they wouldn't be observed by those who had just arrived and within a short time they were well away from the castle and headed toward Collinwood.

As they reached the entrance of the mansion they turned back and saw the flames from the castle. It was burning down, but still remained a spectacular sight.

Her eyes fixed on it, she said, "I'll never forget tonight."

"I can well believe it," Barnabas said. "And when you go inside, I want you to remember that you may still be in danger. Bentley created a number of those zombies. One or more of them may still be at large with orders to harm you."

She gasped. "You think that possible?"

"I do," he said solemnly.

She gazed up at him. "Won't you come inside with me?"

He shook his head. "No. Not the way things are. I'll probably see you later."

"What will I say about the castle and what happened there?"

"Try to avoid talking about it," he said. "If they ask where you were, tell them you decided to remain overnight at the old house as my guest."

She nodded. "I will."

They kissed and she went into the silence of the house. She mounted the stairs and went down the dark hallway to her bedroom. Barnabas had made her wary with his talk of danger. And in the stillness of the ancient mansion she began to feel uneasy once again. The terror might not be over. This could be only a lull.

She stepped into her bedroom and saw that a candle had been set out for her and the bed turned down. She supposed that James and Maria Collins, along with the servants, had all gone over to observe the burning castle at close range. The house might be deserted except for herself. Her nerves became more on edge.

She crossed to the dresser and was about to begin undressing for bed when she heard the door from the hallway open. She turned in fear and surprise to see John Williams standing in the open doorway.

Then she gave a gasp of relief. "John! I couldn't imagine who it was! I thought you'd gone over to the fire with the others."

The haggard face of the young doctor showed no expression. "Bentley is dead, isn't he?"

"Yes. But I'm going to pretend to know nothing about it," she said. She had gone over to him and was facing him now. His eyes held a strange gleam and he seemed to be trembling.

"Now you must die," he announced in a cold voice.

"John!" She stepped back in horror. "Are you mad?"

"You must die!" He sprang forward and seized her throat.

She felt the mad pressure of his strong hands crush her neck. She fell to her knees, a pleading expression on her face. She would die after all…

"Let her go!" She vaguely heard the words shouted in the familiar resonant voice of Barnabas. At the same time the cruel hands released her and she slumped back on the floor. Barnabas was in the room, holding up a cross in his left hand. And John Williams had shrunk back and was cowering before the cross.

Barnabas stood over him sternly. "You are Bentley's slave, aren't you?" he demanded. "You have been since he captured you in London. He pretended to let you go free. But the John Williams he freed was not the living one but a zombie, murdered and conditioned to do his bidding. Do you deny it?"

Johns' haggard face was distorted by fear. He made a whimpering sound and with a last frantic glance at her, he turned and ran out into the hallway. Barnabas followed him, his cape flowing and the cross held high.

She dragged herself up into a chair, her throat aching and her mind still unable to accept the horror of what had taken place. She sat there for several minutes in the shadowed room, wondering what was happening. Then from high above in the upper part of the mansion she heard what sounded like a banshee scream. A long wailing cry!

Getting to her feet, she went out into the hallway. By the time she reached the landing she met Barnabas coming slowly down the stairs. He gave her a sober look as he joined her.

"The book is closed," he said. "John Williams threw himself from the captain's walk to his death! It's over! The last of Bentley's evil has been destroyed."

Her eyes were wide. "How will we explain it?"

"Williams was in bad health," Barnabas said. "Everyone knows he seemed a little mad since his wife's death. They'll consider it a suicide, which it was. He no longer wanted to go on with that zombie existence."

Paula touched a hand wearily to her temple. "Oh, Barnabas, will it ever end?"

"It has ended," he said gently, an arm around her. "I see no reason why you can't return to Widenham Square soon."

"If you will come with me," she said.

"Perhaps," he said. "Now I must try and find someone to look after his body, and you and I shall await the return of the family in the drawing room. Under the circumstances there should be no discussion of my failings."

"I know it was Lily who attacked those girls," she said.

"It was," Barnabas said with a sigh. "But James prefers to think I'm the guilty one. No matter. He'll be too shocked by Williams' suicide to make an issue of it tonight."

This proved true. When James and Maria returned they heard the news of Williams' plunge from the rooftop with consternation. It was almost dawn before Barnabas left and Paula went up to sleep the sleep of the exhausted.

She didn't come downstairs again until late in the afternoon. The excitement of the fire and the suicide still was the talk of the village, she learned from Maria. And it had been assumed that all the occupants of the castle had been caught in the blaze and burned to death.

As dusk arrived she became uneasy. Anxious to talk to Barnabas about what their next move would be, she hurried along the path to the old house as soon as twilight came. When she reached it she was startled to see a loaded wagon outside its doors. And Barnabas and Willie Loomis were standing by it.

She rushed up to Barnabas. "What is happening?"

He looked down at her with tenderness in his deep-set eyes. "I'm leaving," he said. "With the trouble here, I must."

"But there'll be no more attacks now that Lily is dead!" she protested.

"The gossip will linger on," Barnabas said. "This is the only way."

"I'll go with you."

"No." He shook his head. "It's not time yet."

"When?" she asked bleakly.

His hands were on her arms. "In another time. When I have my health."

"I want us to be married now," she insisted.

"It's not possible," Barnabas said quietly. "Go back to Widenham Square. That is where you belong. And who knows? Some misty night you may look out your window and see a familiar figure standing under the yellow of the gaslights. And this time it won't be anyone you need fear. It will be me, come back to you."

Her eyes filled with tears. "You will come back! Promise me!"

Barnabas bent close to her and touched his lips to hers for a farewell kiss. And then without a word he got up on the wagon seat beside Willie. There was a flick of the reins and the horses started away.

Paula remained standing there in the growing darkness, watching until there was no sign of the wagon at all, though she could hear the distant creaking of its wheels taking Barnabas from her. Then, sadly, she turned and began walking back to Collinwood.